A Red War Annals Story

The Crown Warrior of Arribor

Helena Š. George

All Scripture quotations are taken from the KJV.

All Psalter quotations from Scottish Metrical Psalter, 1650.

Cover design © Miblart

Interior formatting by Sarah Rodecker

Chapter Header Art by Joseph Rodecker (@weights_dont_lie)

Map by Sarah Rodecker

No AI was used in the creation of this work.

ISBN: 979-8-9951216-0-2

First Edition

A Red War Annals Story

The Crown Warrior of Arribor

Helena Š. George

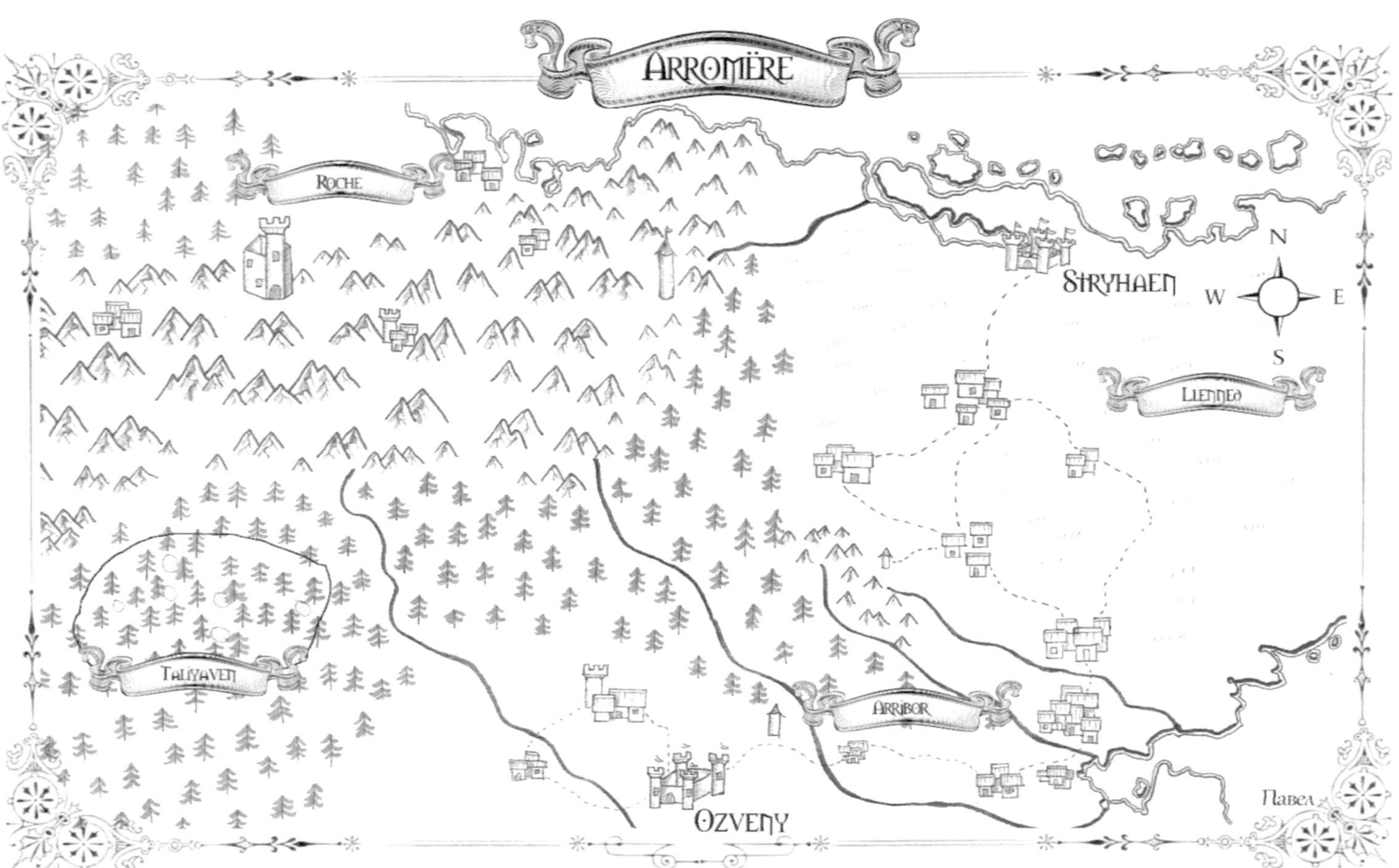
ARROMËRE
ROCHE
STRYHAEN
N
W
E
S
LIENNED
TALIYAVEN
ARRIBOR
OZVENY
Павел

More by the Author

The Red War Annals

The Lost Bard of Taliyaven
The Red Bard of Roche
The Singing Bard of Llenned
The Warrior Bard of Arribor

Red War Annals Stories

The Crown Warrior of Arribor

The Pirate Hunter Chronicles

Ships, Secrets, and Survivors
Sins, Sons, and Siren Songs
Rumors, Reunions, and Revenge
Rogues, Royals, and Raiding Roc
Pirate Hunter Legends

This book is dedicated to my hard-working mother, who taught me self-control and the ability to see through to the end the things that I put my hands to.

PROLOGUE

YULI

SOCHI, ROCHE, SECOND AGE, 1998.

A seagull cried overhead as Yuli perched on a barrel and watched enforcers surround the *Quiet Waters* inn. Smoke rose from the little shrine in the inn's courtyard, tugged about by the icy sea winds, but Yuli now knew that the offerings were only a cover. That fire hadn't been lit with prayers to the gods. He'd even seen it grow cold many times in his past few weeks of spying.

This was his favorite part of the job–finding where the gods were forgotten and making things right again. Places like *Quiet Waters,* where sacrifices were neglected and offering fires ignored, called down the hatred of the gods onto the land.

Roche was already a barren place because of the gods' curses. It was only due to the guidance of the priests that the land was not wholly consumed by fire and ash. Yuli was banned from serving in the priesthood, a fact sealed by the slave tattoo on his cheek, but he could still serve the gods by exposing unbelievers. Anyone who found and reported Christians would be blessed, both in this life and the next, even if they were born slaves.

Claws scratched on wood, and Yuli looked over to see a seagull perched on the barrel beside his own. The bird tilted its head to stare at the fish pie in Yuli's hand.

"It's mine," Yuli said, turning away from the bird. "My master gave it to me as a gift."

Every time Yuli brought word of the whereabouts of Christians, his master rewarded him. Sometimes he offered a few coins or a worn cloak, but Yuli liked it best when the old priest gave him food. As a slave, Yuli wasn't allowed inside the best inns and taverns. But that didn't stop him from standing outside and smelling the food.

Across the street, the enforcers broke the inn door and rushed inside, swords drawn. Yuli knew what they would find inside: a Christian family holding an illegal worship service on a sacrificial morning.

The inn was a perfect cover. With patrons visiting from other lands, the family would have had to remain at work to serve the sailors. The patrons, unfamiliar with the customs of the land, wouldn't notice if the inn received a stream of Rochen visitors who should have been attending the sacrifices at the heart of the city.

When the first terrified scream filled the air, drowning out the nearby gulls, Yuli knew it was time to leave. If word got out that the little boy begging scraps around the shipyard was a slave for the High Priest of Sochi, his spying days would be over.

This was his least favorite part of the job—watching people who had been kind to him die. Sometimes the enforcers killed them on the spot. Other times, the prisoners were kept alive until a market day so everyone could watch them die.

Either way, blood was spilled and the gods would forgive their trespasses. The ocean town of Sochi would be cleansed, and perhaps Yuli would receive another pie or two. These days he was always hungry, and pie kept him full and warm.

The cook at *Quiet Waters* often gave him pie. Whenever she saw him begging in the courtyard, she would call him over and give him something warm to eat. She used to offer him a place by the fire, but once he was certain they were Christians, he had to refuse. Eating food from her hands was bad enough, but stepping under her roof? The gods would never forgive that.

Yuli's stomach growled, and he took a bite of his fish pie. Sailors were streaming out of the inn doors now, fleeing the prospect of watching an execution. Today was their lucky day, for no one would expect them to pay for their drinks now that the proprietor was arrested.

The gull made a grab for the pie, and Yuli chased it away with a wave. After a final glance at the *Quiet Waters*, he hopped off his barrel and made for the harbor. By his estimation, he had enough time to check on one of his other suspected locations and return to the inn before the recorder came to log the raid.

If he timed everything right, there might be a few minutes during which the inn would be completely empty. Patrons gone, owners captured, enforcers hunting down those who escaped. It would be just enough time for Yuli to slip inside and do a small raid of his own. He knew exactly what he would grab.

One of the daughters played the *gusli.* Yuli knew very little about instruments, but its glittering pearl decorations probably meant that one was worth some money. Yuli knew a ship captain that would pay money, questions unasked, for a nice *gusli.*

The daughter certainly wouldn't need it anymore. Yuli would miss hearing her music, like he would miss her mother's steaming hot pies. It was a pity that they chose to anger the gods by worshipping one they couldn't even see. Yuli didn't understand how such kind, smiling people could bring down anger and judgment onto their own home.

He caught a whiff of blood on the wind and picked up his pace. He had done his job, and the gods would bless him for it. The Solovyov family was no longer his concern.

Chapter 1

Anya Solovyova

Ozveny, the Royal City of Arribor, Second Age, 1998.

"Once upon a dreary night,

a cold and wild winter night,

a minstrel came, with music fame,

and knocked upon the door.

She left fresh snow upon the floor,

and set her boots beside the door.

With gusli *bright and voice so light,*

she shared her tale of woe."

Anya sang to the sunrise, her voice raspy from a night of little sleep. Staring at the starlit garden was better than sleeping through nightmares, and now she had a terrific view of the *hrad* towers turning from gray to gleaming white as the sun rose.

She pulled the blanket closer around her shoulders and leaned back against the porch railing. Lights glowed behind the windows of nearby houses as people rose and stoked their fires.

Ozveny, the Royal City of Arribor, was waking up. Anya sniffed and continued in her sing-song whisper.

"A lover gone, abandoned so.

The minstrel cries, Oh death and woe!

As blood is red, and graves hold dead,

my lonely tale is true."

Over two weeks ago, what had started as an ordinary church service had soon become a bloodbath. Christian worship was banned in Roche and, somehow, the priests must have learned that Anya's family held services at their inn.

Some of the Christians were killed trying to escape. Others, like Anya and her father, made it out alive. The rest were captured and publicly executed a few days later.

Because *Quiet Waters* was such a popular place to eat, the locals were particularly distraught at learning they had been served by Christians. The ensuing hunt for survivors was enough to convince Father it was safer to leave Roche than to try and stay hidden. The small group of *Biblia* smugglers they worked with helped them board a ship, where they left everything behind—including Anya's mother.

"You're up early."

Anya looked up to see Father crossing the garden. Their hosts had erected a temporary home out of the garden shed, giving Anya and her father a bit of unexpected privacy. Compared to sharing a cramped room in a ship with ten other people, or trying to find sleep in a bumpy cart, the garden shed was quiet and spacious.

"Did you have another nightmare?" Father asked, taking a seat on the porch beside Anya and sliding an arm behind her shoulders.

The memories of Vera's death had frequently haunted Anya's nights since the day of the raid. If she closed her eyes, she could still see her sister kneeling in a patch of snow with her hands tied behind her back. If she let her mind and hands grow idle, she could see the bloody sword piercing Vera's heart.

"*Da,*" Anya said, rubbing her eyes. "I couldn't sleep, so I came out here so I wouldn't wake you."

"A garden is one of the best places to watch the sunrise." Father took a deep breath and sighed. "Let me go in the house and see if there is hot water for tea. Wait here."

Anya waited, her hands resting useless in her lap. She needed something to do, or else her mind would wander...

She didn't want to remember blood dripping onto snow.

She didn't want to remember death lurking behind the eyes of the man holding the sword.

She didn't want to remember the tattoos marking the man as a silencer.

She didn't want to remember the way the crowd cheered as the silencer cut through the group of Christians.

She didn't want to remember, but she did anyway. There was nothing else to do. Back home, she would have risen before the sun to prepare the inn with the rest of her family. Breakfast at *Quiet Waters* needed to be prepared before their customers woke. Horses had to be fed and readied for departure.

The Solovyov family didn't dare risk hiring servants, lest word get out that they were Christians. That meant they did all the work themselves. Mother cooked, Father saw to the stables, and Anya and her little sister Vera did everything in between.

Father returned to the porch with two cups of tea. Anya gratefully took the offered drink, breathing in the relaxing steam. She pushed away a lingering memory of blood and dead eyes and turned back to the sunrise.

"We made it," Father said. "Our first morning in Ozveny."

"Not all of us made it," Anya replied.

Vera was dead. Some of the other Christians caught worshipping at *Quiet Waters* had been killed with her. The ones left alive would surely be sent to the Games of Silence, where their painful deaths would be inevitable.

Only Mother's fate remained unknown. She had fled with some of the children, and no one had heard from them since. The smugglers had promised to find her and send her on the next ship.

Anya could only hope they were able to keep their promise. She looked at her fingers, feeling the calluses beneath her thumb. She'd left so many things behind in Roche—her books, her beloved *gusli*, her new boots. But she would gladly never see them again if it meant Mother would live.

"Perhaps we should go for a walk while we drink our tea," Father suggested. "Sitting here and doing nothing will not ease our fears. And I want to look at all those gardens."

Father hated being still. Anya understood his need for movement. Wandering through the strange city couldn't be as dangerous as hiding for their lives in Roche.

The sun continued to rise as Anya and her father stepped onto the road and began their walk. This early in the morning, they appeared to be the only souls out and about. Dew coated the moss-covered stone walls and sparkled on flowerbeds.

Roche was a dreary land, full of black earth and gray stone. There were no trees, and greenery only grew where it was carefully tended. Only the wealthy had enough money and servants to afford gardens.

Arribor was *alive*. Trees grew in the fields and valleys. Flowers bloomed beside every house and cottage. The air smelled clear, and warm winds promised a beautiful summer.

Anya tried to hate it. She walked past beautiful gardens and houses while her sister lay dead in some unmarked grave. She lived in quiet and safety while her mother remained missing. How could she enjoy herself when every breath ached with the pain of loss?

"Any word about Mother?" The words slipped from Anya's lips. She knew the answer. It was the same as it had been for weeks.

Her father shook his head. "The next *Biblia* smuggler ship was supposed to sail out two weeks after we did. If she's on it, we won't know until they reach land."

Anya didn't want to wait two weeks for news. She wanted to know *now.* "I hope she's all right. The smugglers said they would find her, but what if they don't?"

"We should never have left Roche." Father stopped and took a sip of his tea. A long moment passed before he spoke again. "I should not have listened to the others and let them convince me. There is nothing for us in Arribor."

He's right. We should never have come here. Anya took a sip of her tea and found it was already cool. She'd hardly drunk any of it. The temptation to fling it to the ground was strong, but she forced her grip on the handle to soften.

It was not her cup. She was a guest living off the kindness of others. The Rochen *Biblia* smugglers had contacts across all of Arromëre, and some Arriborn nobles were willing to open their homes (and their garden sheds) to help Christians in need.

"I've never seen so many flowers." Father pointed to a house on their right. A stone walk led the way from the road to the front door, surrounded by rosebushes and small trees. "I've wanted to do something like that in front of the inn for years."

Roses were expensive to buy and difficult to keep alive once in the ground. Sometimes it seemed like the very dirt of Roche was determined to keep things of beauty from thriving.

"I think it would look pretty with roses out front." Anya swallowed a wave of sorrow. They might never stand outside *Quiet Waters* again. Someone else would run the inn. Someone else would tend to travelers. Their former livelihood was gone.

She took a few quick sips of the cold tea and turned to study the next house. More flowers. More green. More proclamations of wealth and happiness.

God, forgive my attitude. These are probably nice people living here. It's not their fault my family is broken. It's not their fault that Arribor is green and Roche is not.

"What happened here?" Father crossed the road to survey another garden. "It's a disaster!"

Anya wasn't much of a gardener, but she could instantly see this one was different from the others. There was no apparent pattern in how things were planted. Cracked stone that had once been part of a walkway jutted amongst weeds and flowers desperate to live.

Father bent to pull a few weeds by the gate, and Anya held her teacup in both hands and looked over the fence to the house beyond. It was just as tall and grand as the surrounding homes, but a distinct air of abandonment hung over it. The chimney was empty of smoke, the shutters were closed, and dead winter leaves molded in heaps by the front door.

Looking at the ivy hanging over the fence, Anya sensed that no one had lived in this house for a long time. If the outside was any indication, the inside must be completely uninhabitable. The roof appeared fine from where she stood, but she could easily imagine holes and deterioration on the other side.

Anya looked back down at her father, only to find him gone. *Captured.*

She gripped her teacup and looked up and down the street. No one. Not even a hint of movement. Father couldn't have been arrested and dragged away without her noticing. He wouldn't have left her alone.

So where had he gone?

Anya waited a moment, a prayer on her lips, then she heard him muttering to himself...from somewhere *inside* the garden. They hadn't been in Ozveny for even a full day, and he was already trespassing—merely to pull weeds!

Then again, the gate *had* been left open, and no one seemed to care about the house anyway. After the past few weeks of mourning and traveling, doing something with his hands would be good for her father.

At first, Anya hesitated to follow him. One person getting thrown into an Arriborn prison was bad enough. But the longer she stared at the gloomy house, the more decisive she became. No one was inside.

As the nearby homes awoke, the smells of smoke and breakfast filled the air. Dogs barked. Someone passed by on the road, whistling a tune. But she found no signs of movement or life beyond the curtains of the abandoned house.

"You can't be here much longer, Father." Anya gathered her courage and passed through the gate into the wild garden. "People are waking up. They'll see you."

"I won't be long, Annushka. Let me clear the way for these roses. There're so many!"

Anya stood and watched for a while, but as the minutes passed, she realized Father was not going to leave anytime soon. She set her teacup on a moss-covered stone bench and knelt on one of the cracked stepping stones. While she wasn't as familiar with flowers as her father, she could at least pull out the half-brown grass growing between the stone cracks.

Wet earth quickly coated her fingers and caked beneath her nails. She welcomed the feeling, tossing handfuls of grass into a pile to the side. If she kept her gaze on the task in front of her and avoided looking at the strange house looming above her, she could pretend she was back in Roche, preparing the inn for the rush of summer guests.

Forget her sister was dead. Forget her mother was missing. Forget she was no longer in her homeland.

She was working. That's all she needed to think about. Eventually, the sound of hooves on the road would signal travelers approaching, and she would jump to her feet, wipe her hands on her apron, and welcome them to the *Quiet Waters.* Vera would prepare hot bowls of soup. And, once the sky grew dark and all the chores were finished, Anya would tune her *gusli* and play a few songs.

That was all. Nothing had changed. She was only working.

Anya risked looking up and saw she'd almost arrived at the front porch. Once she reached it, she would call it a day and drag her father away. Their hosts had to be wondering where they were by now, and they had a big day ahead of them.

She looked back over her shoulder to see her handiwork and had no time to admire the cleaned stepping stones. A squeak left her mouth, not even loud enough to warn her father.

A man stood at the garden entrance, one gloved hand on the gate. A black handkerchief covered his nose and mouth, revealing only a pale forehead and black eyes. The long hilt of a two-handed sword stuck out over his left shoulder.

After not even a full day in Ozveny, Anya and her father would be arrested. What did they do to Rochen in Arribor? Would they be sent back home? Killed on the spot?

Anya noted two more swords hanging from the stranger's belt, and her heart sank. *Killed on the spot* seemed far more likely.

A memory of Vera kneeling before the silencer gave Anya the courage she needed to face the stranger and fall to her knees. "If you're going to kill us, please make it quick."

Chapter 2

Anya Solovyova

Lozveny, the Royal City of Arribor, Second Age, 1998.

The stranger stared at Anya, then at her father. He crouched before a patch of weeds, his hands frozen in the act of pulling up the invaders.

Had someone seen them and called for an arrest? Was this man going to drag them off to some dark prison? They didn't have Games of Silence in Arribor. No trained silencers willing to kill on command. So, what happened to prisoners?

"I'm sorry," Father said, rising and brushing dirt from his knees. "We should not have trespassed, but we meant no harm. We'll be on our way."

"Ah'm not goin' tae hurt ye," the man spoke. His strange accent was muffled behind the handkerchief. "Ye can care fer the flowers if ye want."

It took Anya a moment to translate the words. The strange pronunciations and the handkerchief made understanding rather difficult. If she were taking his *pivo* order in a crowded room, she would have to ask him to repeat himself. Maybe multiple times.

They stared at each other for a moment, then the stranger entered the garden, carefully stepping on each newly cleared stepping stone. "Ah want tae ken why ye're in mae garden."

Anya stared at the pile of weeds at their feet and wondered if she'd somehow misunderstood his words. Could he really not see what terrible shape his garden was in?

Wait. *His* garden?

"This is your house?" Anya asked.

The man nodded. "*Áno.* An' ye're in mae garden."

Anya studied the swords at the man's side and the one on his back. His boots were worn but well-made, and the cloak slung over his shoulder flashed with gold threads. He did not appear to be poor. There was no reason for his house to be as run-down as it was.

"We're in your garden because no one takes care of it," Anya said. "The flowers are dying."

"Ah see flowers. They look alive."

Father raised his handful of weeds. "The weeds aren't dying either. How are you supposed to walk to the front door in all this mess?"

"Ah gae in the back door."

"What about your guests?" Anya had seen the smaller, poorer houses farther in the city and she compared them to this house. This house was for the wealthy. Wealthy people had parties.

"Ah donnae have guests."

Her original prediction aside, she wasn't surprised. No self-respecting wealthy person would visit such an abandoned place. The neighbors probably hated the sight of it. "Well, your garden is a mess. You need to do something about it."

"Ah'm sorry."

Anya couldn't tell if he was serious in his apology, or teasing. The handkerchief over his face hid most of his expressions–if he had any at all. His glance was restless, constantly flicking from Anya to Father to the garden and to the road beside them.

"I'm sorry we bothered you." Father put his hand on Anya's shoulder and gave a meaningful push in the direction of the gate. "We will leave now. This won't happen again."

Anya spread her skirt in a polite curtsy, the way she'd greeted rich customers at the inn. "Good morning." Her voice was friendly, but she put a different message in her eyes. *Please, please, please let us leave without causing a fuss.*

The stranger bowed in return. "Thank ye fer takin' care of mae garden." He made no move to stop them as they hurried through the gate.

Once they were in the safety of the road and out of earshot, Father brushed the last bit of dirt from his hands. "We should have been more careful. I thought no one lived there."

"He didn't seem angry about it." Anya risked a glance back. The street was empty. *Good.*

"That's not my concern." Father lowered his voice. "If he'd found out we were from Roche, we might have been in more danger. It's only been seven years since the war. I doubt the Arriborns have forgotten or forgiven Roche for attacking them."

He was right, of course. Even though a tentative peace had been arranged between Arribor and Roche, that didn't mean old wounds were already forgotten.

This stranger carried swords with the practiced ease of a warrior. There was no way he hadn't fought in the war. He would have killed Rochen. His friends, maybe even family, would have been killed by Rochen hands. It was best they stay far away from him and anyone else who might harbor hatred for Roche.

Father took Anya's hand. "Well, that's that. Let's go back before our hosts worry about us."

Anya realized she'd left the teacup behind in the garden, but she was *not* going back to retrieve it.

CHAPTER 3

ANYA SOLOVYOVA

LOZVENY, THE ROYAL CITY OF ARRIBOR, SECOND AGE, 1998.

"We found a place for you to stay." Ružena Rehák nudged her husband with an elbow and bounced on the edge of the couch they shared. "I think it will be perfect!"

Anya glanced at the husband, a man clad in a warrior's tunic, and wondered if he had lost friends to Rochen swords. He seemed to hold no hatred for the Rochen currently lodged in his house and had even played a game of chess with Father last night.

"There's an Arriborn noble needing a housekeeper," Ružena continued. "Both you and your father can live there in exchange for managing the house. He will also pay."

This was better than anything Anya had prayed for. A job, a place to stay, *and* at the same place as her father. Was it faithless that she hadn't even bothered to pray for such a thing? She leaned on her father's shoulder and let out a sigh. "Perfect!"

"God has blessed us," Father bowed his head towards Ružena. "We cannot thank you enough for all you have done for us. And for the others."

"I'll take you there this evening." Ružena glanced out the window, where two small children played in the front gardens with a puppy, then turned back to Anya and her father. "I've found a place for Yekaterina to stay as well, and getting her situated will take most of the day, I expect."

It wasn't necessarily Anya's business, but the fate of her friend still interested her. "Where is she going?"

"An old friend of mine owns a bakery. She's agreed to let Yekaterina work there for a while and become...familiar with working."

At first glance, Anya could see that Ružena was also a pampered noble like Yekaterina. Her home was large and clean and her clothes colorful and of high quality. She carried herself with an air of importance and could even read and write.

But Anya watched her hands.

Ružena's hands were never still. She'd pulled up a few weeds as she'd walked to the garden shed and back to the house. She'd wiped down the kitchen table with a damp cloth as she'd made arrangements for her Rochen guests. And now, as she sat on the couch with her husband and guests, she sewed a tear in an embroidered vest.

Ružena was comfortable with work. Anya liked her.

"Pack your things," Ružena said. "When I return, I'll take you to your new home."

They didn't have much to pack. Anya had fled her home with only the clothes on her back. Having no money, she and her father made the journey to Arribor only through the kindness and efforts of the *Biblia* smugglers. Father had found things to do on the ship to earn a bit of money for emergencies.

Anya knew they could never repay those who risked their lives to help the Christians in Roche. Persecution didn't exist on this side of the mountains, yet people willingly traveled to Roche to support their Christian family. Perhaps someday, Anya could return the kindness.

Ružena returned late, as expected. The look she gave Anya explained the results more than words could. Yekaterina was going to take a while to adjust to her new situation.

"You said your family took care of an inn?" Ružena asked as they left the garden shed behind and began their walk up the road.

"*Áno*, we did. It was started by my great-grandfather," Father said proudly. "He built it close to the harbor, and we had visitors from all over the known world. It's why we speak so many languages and why Anya plays all kinds of songs."

Anya missed the place, and not only the familiarity. She missed having something to do. At the *Quiet Waters*, she'd always had a customer to care for, dishes to clean, places to sweep. She'd spent this afternoon washing the floors in Ružena's kitchen merely to keep her hands and mind occupied.

"That's what we thought. I sensed this would be a good place for you. Kazimír agreed. Dmitriy was unsure at first, but I think he'll see that his place needs your presence."

"Are there other servants?"

"*Nie.* It will only be you and your father. Hence Dmitriy's need for a caretaker."

That didn't sound too bad. "I will be glad to work again."

"I completely understand."

The not-abandoned house appeared on their left, and Anya wondered if her teacup was still sitting on the bench. Maybe she could duck inside the garden to grab it? She hated to lose it, especially after Ružena had been so kind to them.

"It looks bad on the outside," Ružena said, directing her steps toward the very gate Anya had walked through earlier that morning. "But it's fine inside. The previous owner let things run wild, even before he passed away. Dmitriy inherited it a few years ago and has done his best to make the place livable again."

"He's not done a good job in the garden," Anya said, turning back to glance at Father. "It definitely needs some work."

"*Áno,*" Father said as they passed the fence and took a small alley path around the side of the house. "It's full of weeds."

"And that's why I thought you two would be perfect for the job. You've done nothing but clean my house and care for my garden since you arrived." Ružena beamed. "It's a perfect fit!"

Anya was strangely torn. Dmitriy had been kind and courteous to them earlier that day, especially considering he'd found them trespassing in his garden. Offering them a place to stay and paying them for their work was beyond generous.

On the other hand, he was a warrior and looked vaguely terrifying. The moment he learned they were Rochen, he would surely withdraw his offer and kick them out onto the streets.

"Does he know...does he know we're from Roche?" Anya asked.

Ružena nodded. "I told him. You don't need to worry. He's been made aware of the situation."

"But...you're *sure*?" Anya tried to forget about the swords. Lots of customers had come to the inn with swords, and it hadn't bothered her. Of course, customers rarely carried *three* swords.

What if this warrior who carried three swords decided he no longer wanted Rochen staying in his house?

"He's rarely home." Ružena waved a hand. "You probably won't see him for days at a time."

"Does he travel much?" That would explain the state of his house and gardens.

"Sometimes. He works and has many other things that keep him from home." Ružena stood in front of the back door and sighed. "I suspect he might come home more frequently if it were a nicer place. He hasn't even invited us over *once* since he moved in."

So Anya's suspicion about the lack of parties was correct.

"I suppose you need a quick tour and instructions." Ruženа gestured to the back courtyard. "This is his. The barn is empty for now, but if you run out of things to do, you could always see about fixing it up. It might be worth the time to acquire a goat or some chickens so you don't have to buy milk and eggs."

The inside of the house was cleaner than Anya expected. A dying fire smoldered in the clay oven, and a drying plate and knife lay on the cooking table. Someone had cooked and eaten something recently. Ružena brazenly opened all the cupboards, sighing at the contents and giving Anya sad, meaningful looks.

Anya stared at the empty shelves and wondered what the master of the house had eaten earlier. Maybe he'd made a fire and used hot water to clean the plate just for fun.

"This is why he never comes home," Ružena said. "There's nothing here. If he had someone keeping the place for him, he wouldn't have to look elsewhere for food."

The kitchen itself was of good quality. A layer of dust and dirt coated some of the surfaces, while others, such as one end of a bench and a corner of the table, appeared to see frequent use.

Father bent to study the fire and poked at a pile of bones. "Squirrel," he said after a moment, his nose wrinkled. "Or rather, it was a squirrel."

A nobleman ate squirrels? Anya shared Ružena's expression of disgust.

"There's a fairly nice sitting room over here." Ružena beckoned them out of the kitchen. "The previous owners often entertained guests. Lady Radovan was especially fond of tea parties. I spent many afternoons here as a little girl."

So that explained Ružena's familiarity with the place.

"When the Radovans passed away, the house was all but abandoned for years. The *kráľ* recently gave it to Dmitriy, partly as a gift and partly to keep the place from completely falling apart."

"A gift from the *kráľ*? That sounds important." Anya tried to imagine the masked and heavily-armed Dmitriy standing before the Arriborn *kráľ*, bowing politely and receiving the gift of a run-down house. Somehow, she couldn't quite picture it.

"Not really. The Nobility Council was pressing him to do something about it, so he did. I think he chose to give it to Dmitriy because it would annoy them. He's petty like that."

The sitting room *was* nice. Cloth was draped over chairs and tables, protecting them from dust, but even with the curtains closed and the fireplace cold and dead, Anya could tell the place would be quite splendid once cared for.

"Your bedrooms will be upstairs. Dmitriy left some money in case you need to purchase anything. I admittedly haven't been upstairs in years, so I'm not sure what we'll find. Dmitriy said he hadn't touched anything." Ružena stopped on the stairs. "Oh, he did say one thing. No one is to go into the study downstairs. And stay out of the west bedroom. Both rooms are off-limits."

"The study. The west bedroom. Understood." Anya nodded.

Ružena turned on the step and leaned down. "I need you to understand how important that is. Dmitriy doesn't say such things lightly. If he doesn't want you in there, you should not go in. I apologize if I've only stirred your curiosity, but promise me you'll leave those rooms alone."

Anya glanced over her shoulder at her father, who nodded. "We promise."

But Ružena was right. Anya's curiosity *had* been stirred.

Chapter 4

Anya Solovyova

Ozveny, the Royal City of Arribor, Second Age, 1998.

As it turned out, they did need to buy things. Lots of things. And it was too late in the day to make it to the market district, or so Ružena had claimed. The noblewoman had apologized greatly and offered to bring blankets and a meal just to help get them through the night.

Father said they would be fine, and Anya tried to explain that dusty blankets were preferrable to sharing a single salty blanket on a freezing ship. The almost-empty house was quieter and safer than conditions they had recently endured, and Anya was ready to settle down.

In the end, Ružena listened and eventually bid them good night, leaving them alone in the house. Once the woman was gone, Father marched into the kitchen and began stoking the fire.

"Supper first, then we'll sleep. Tomorrow, we'll survey the situation. Can you check outside? I thought I saw firewood stacked out back."

Anya brought in firewood, re-scoured all the empty cupboards (in case she'd missed something the first time), then carried the dusty blankets from the sitting room into the courtyard to shake them off in the last light of the setting sun.

It almost felt like they had been given a house. If Ružena was right—that Dmitriy was rarely home and held little interest in how things were cared for—they would be free to manage the house how they liked. Anya liked having that freedom. She knew Father would too. They had managed the *Quiet Waters* for far too long to easily settle down and work for someone else.

Perhaps Ružena knew that. God certainly knew, and He was in control of this entire situation.

Their supper was meager—three old potatoes Anya had found lurking in a corner of the kitchen. They cooked them in the clay oven and ate them with an abundance of thankfulness and no seasoning.

"Our first meal alone since...since we were discovered." Father scooted the bench a little closer to the oven. "I've missed the peace and quiet."

There hadn't been much peace and quiet at *Quiet Waters*. Customers had come and gone—some only for a meal, others to stay the night. Even when the inn had been empty, there'd been rooms to clean and other chores to be done. But after weeks of strangers and strange languages and strange places, their need for a quiet place was sharp.

"We'll take inventory tomorrow and see what we need to purchase." Anya studied the pouch of money left on the table. They hadn't counted the contents yet, and Dmitriy had not told Ružena how much it held. "Food, most importantly."

"Gardening tools," Father added.

Of course the wild garden was Father's most important concern. He would be almost useless in the house until the outside was cleared to his satisfaction.

All the better. Then he wouldn't be in the way while Anya saw to cleaning the inside. She would need to dust. Thankfully, it was warm outside and she could open the windows.

The door to the kitchen banged open, and Dmitriy entered, carrying two steaming bowls. He stared at the two occupants for a moment, then kicked the door closed with a booted toe. "Ah have soup," he said.

He moved silently across the kitchen floor, his shoulder dipping with a slight limp, and set the bowls on the table. "Are ye hungry?"

The few potatoes *had* been very small.

"There isn't much to eat in the kitchen," Anya said.

"Ah ken." Dmitriy gestured to the bowls. "So Ah brought ye soup."

Anya wanted to ask where the soup had come from, but Father had already taken a bowl and was bowing his head over it in prayer. She doubted Ružena would have placed them in a home of someone who would be inclined to poison them, so she took the other bowl, prayed, then thanked Dmitriy.

Their new employer stood and watched them for a moment, still as a stone statue. Anya wasn't even sure he blinked. Then he pulled his gloves off, set a pot of water on the oven to heat, and gathered the used plates.

"Oh, you don't need to do that!" Anya jumped up. "That's why you hired us. We're doing the cleaning from now on."

Dmitriy paused, studied the plates, then set them down. "Ah understand. Sorry." He picked up his gloves, and the movement caught Anya's attention. He was missing part of a finger on his right hand.

A missing finger. A limp. The handkerchief covering his face. Three swords. Some sort of friendship with the *kráľ* that had earned him a house he rarely used. A willingness to hire strangers, even after he knew they were Rochen.

And now soup.

What a strange man.

"I'll clean the kitchen when we're done. Don't worry about it. Please." Anya put her hands on her hips. "It's my job."

Dmitriy pulled his gloves on and bowed. "Very well. Ah understand. Leave the bowls. Ah'll return them tomorrow."

Then he limped to the door and walked out into the night.

Chapter 5

Anya Solovyova

Ozveny, the Royal City of Arribor, Second Age, 1998.

Shopping was not as daunting as Anya thought it would be. Most people were friendly, and no one noticed her occasional hesitation as she spoke their language. The money Dmitriy had left them was more than enough for filling the kitchen cupboards and purchasing a few blankets and pillows for their beds.

Anya did take a minute to look at fabric and other clothing options. She didn't dare use the provided money for something so personal, but once she had her own spending money, she would be buying another dress, or at least a nice apron. Once she had a decent grasp on prices and how much she would need to save, she returned to her new home.

Father was outside in the garden, as she expected. He waved a dirty hand at her, and she smiled back. The garden would keep him happy and occupied for the next few days. It wouldn't be enough to make the grief and fear go away, but at least he wouldn't be alone with his thoughts.

Anya planned to occupy her own thoughts with work as well.

She spent the day cleaning the kitchen. Every corner was dusted and washed, and a few bits of old or suspicious food were thrown into a newly made burn pile in the back courtyard. She organized and stored the new purchases in the cupboards.

As expected, the time passed quickly. Anya made dinner, which she shared with her father. Dmitriy never made an appearance, so they cleaned up and went to bed.

In the morning, they discovered money left on the table, along with a note. Anya held it by the kitchen fire to read, nearly setting it alight. The handwriting was fairly legible, much to her relief.

Speaking another language was one skill, but reading in another language was completely different.

Your first pay, the letter read. *Buy what you need. Thank you for cleaning the house. I will pay at the end of every week.*

Anya counted the money twice and wondered if this would be the rate for every week, or if Dmitriy had taken into account they were only working two days this week. If this was the pay for two days, she was satisfied. But if this was what they were going to earn every week?

Would Ružena be offended if they searched for a different job and housing situation? Anya set down the money and shook her head. She would worry about that later. The neglected sitting room was calling her name...

Ružena dropped in that night and gave them directions to the *hrad* church. She also brought freshly baked cookies and a small basket of clothes. “A donation from the church. I thought these might fit you. Are you settling in?”

Anya nodded. “*Áno.* Thanks for checking on us.”

“Has Dmitriy been by?”

“Once. Twice, actually. We never saw him the second time, but he paid us.”

“Good. If he forgets to pay you, come find me. I don’t think he will, but he is pretty busy, and he’s never had to worry about someone depending on him like this before.”

“What does he do that keeps him so busy?” Anya had the feeling it had something to do with the swords. No one carried three swords around unless they needed them. It was far too much steel just for show.

“He works in the *hrad* as a Crown Warrior.”

“Crown Warrior?”

“A personal bodyguard to the royal family, which is currently only the *kráľ*. But Dmitriy has lots of friends here in Ozveny, and I think they take advantage of him. He’s always running around helping with one thing or another.” Ružena laughed. “If you can, try to get him to rest. I don’t think he knows how to be still.”

Anya understood that, at least a little. Running an inn often didn’t leave much time for resting. There always was something that needed to be done, and even when quiet moments appeared, Anya preferred to play music.

Music. That was something else Anya needed to save for. There had to be somewhere in the city she could buy an instrument. A *gusli* was preferrable, but she would willingly play anything she could afford.

A house wasn't a real home until it held an instrument. Music helped calm nerves worn down from a day of hard labor, made the cold winter nights pass with ease, and brought smiles and laughter into a place that had once been dreary.

Anya saw Ružena out, then returned to the kitchen to find Father was already raiding the cookies. They shared them by the fire and sang a few songs. It was the happiest Anya had felt since her family had been torn apart.

In the morning, she cooked *pirohy* and set some out in case Dmitriy came home. Then she left with her father for the church Ružena had recommended. It was small, as Ružena had said, which meant their presence would not go unnoticed. Anya had to repeat her name and reason for visiting many times before everyone took their seats in the pews and the service began.

The singing stole Anya's breath away. Voices of men and women and children rose in harmony, cheerful and joyous as they sang the opening *žalm.*

"The Lord is just in all his ways,

holy in his works all.

God's near to all that call on him,

in truth that on him call."

Father grabbed Anya's hand and squeezed it. He was not able to read the common tongue and join in the singing, but he could listen and understand the words. In time, he might master the letters and be able to follow along.

Not that Anya expected to stay in Arribor that long. If her mother wasn't on the next ship, she suspected Father would want to return to Roche and find her. Anya did not want to be left behind.

"He will accomplish the desire

of those that do him fear:

He also will deliver them,

and he their cry will hear.

The Lord preserves all who him love,

that naught can them annoy:

But he all those that wicked are

will utterly destroy."

As the *žalm* continued, Anya found her gaze wandering over the heads of the people standing in front of her. A sea of dark hair, broken only by colorful headscarves worn by women, swam before her. She tucked a finger under her own scarf, ensuring it hadn't come loose, and a sudden flash of black caught her attention.

Dmitriy stood in the front row on the far side, between the end of the pew and the wall. He carried his swords and wore the usual black handkerchief across his face. The young man sitting at the end of the pew beside him bore a thin golden circlet on his brow and sang with emotion, his shoulders rising with every breath and elbows jerking at the beginning of each verse.

If Dmitriy was a royal bodyguard, did that mean the young man beside him was the *král*? He looked very young–too young to be wearing a crown and carrying the weight of a throne.

Of course, the recent war had taken many lives, and royalty were not exempt from death. How many members of the royal family had died so that this young man could claim the throne?

"My mouth the praises of the Lord

to publish cease shall never:

Let all flesh bless his holy name

for ever and for ever."

The singing ended, and Anya sat back down in the pew with the others. When a man stood in the pulpit and opened the *Biblia*, Anya turned away to focus on the minister. She was here to worship, not stare at strangers.

How young the *kráľ* of Arribor was and how he'd gained the throne was none of her business. Right now, she was a stranger. A visitor. Arriborn politics were nothing she needed to meddle in.

Chapter 6

Anya Solovyova

Ozveny, the Royal City of Arribor, Second Age, 1998.

Monday morning brought a torrent of warm spring rain, and Anya opened the windows of the sitting room to let the smell of flowers and earth fill the house. Father, chased inside by the rain, busied himself with mending the holes in their donated clothes. He sang as he worked, and Anya, who was sweeping in the sitting room, hummed along with him.

She found a *gusli* under the couch, discovered only because she'd pushed the couch to the side to sweep underneath and heard the sudden *zing* of untuned strings. Anya recognized the sound instantly and eagerly bent to inspect the instrument.

The *gusli* was in good condition, despite being covered in dust and bearing a worn set of strings. Anya decided the sweeping could be finished later and plunked herself onto the floor with the *gusli* in her lap—tuning, plucking, and tuning again.

When she finally looked up, she found Father standing in the doorway, tears trailing down his cheeks. "It reminds me of home," he whispered. "I didn't realize how much I missed hearing you play until now."

Anya had missed playing, but now that her fingers were aching, she realized just how long it had been since she had held an instrument. With *gusli* strings under her fingertips, she could imagine she was back in Roche, back at the *Quiet Waters,* playing a tune for weary travelers while her mother cleaned a nearby tabletop and her sister carried out another tray of honey cookies.

Burning tears slid down Anya's face, and she reached a hand up to wipe them away. "I miss home," she whispered. "I wish we hadn't left. I wish the priests had never caught wind of the services at the inn. I wish the enforcers had never come."

"I know." Father closed his eyes. "I wish that every night."

Time couldn't be reversed. There was no way to go back and do things differently. Vera was dead. Mother was missing.

Anya turned her attention back to the *gusli.* The instrument itself was well-made and, once it had a new set of strings, would sound beautiful. It couldn't hold a candle to the one Anya had left in Roche, but she had saved her money for almost five years to make that purchase.

Would buying new strings for this *gusli* be included under her regular housekeeping duties? Or should she save her own money? Perhaps she could split it. After all, it was Dmitriy's instrument, but she would be the one playing it.

Did Dmitriy play the *gusli*? Was it his? Or perhaps it had come with the house. Perhaps he didn't even know it existed.

Well, the next time she saw him, she would ask. She couldn't imagine him playing an instrument—or even enjoying music at all. Warriors were a different sort of people. In Roche, joining the Army was a point of pride. Everyone hoped their children would qualify, not only for the money gained but for the boasting privileges.

The Games of Darkness had once been held for all to participate in. The brave could enter themselves and fight for glory. The poor would raise their swords in a valiant effort to gain a better place in life. But now, only slaves were allowed to fight in the arenas, giving their blood for money only their masters would see. Freeborns who wanted to carry the sword and fight their way to glory had only one choice—joining Roche's Army.

None of it was right. The past and present Games only encouraged the bloodlust that filled the veins of the Rochen people. It showed their need to break free of the chains and lies that the priests and fake gods wrapped them in.

Another reason Anya needed to return. The *Quiet Waters* had been more than a family business. It was a place Christians could meet in safety. The Solovyov family had helped hide and transport messages and *Biblias* and traveling ministers.

Anya set the *gusli* on the couch. "I'll see about something to eat," she said. The instrument wasn't hers to worry about. She wouldn't be here long enough to go through a new set of strings.

Dmitriy was in the kitchen when Anya walked in. He hunkered in front of the oven, holding a small object on a stick over the flames. His cloak hung over a chair, and the three swords lay across the table. The smell of burning meat filled the kitchen.

"I didn't realize you were home," Anya said. "I'm sorry I don't have anything ready to eat yet."

"Ah have somethin'," Dmitriy said, tilting his head toward the spitted animal in the oven. "Ye donna need tae worry about me."

"I'm the housekeeper. It's my job to prepare your meals. I was about to start cooking."

Dmitriy scooted over a little. "Ye need me tae move?"

Anya bent over and stared into the oven. "What are you cooking?"

"Squirrel."

"... *Why?*"

Dmitriy pulled the stick out, surveyed the little body, and put it back in the oven. "Quick tae kill an' eat. Caught it on mae way home from the barracks."

"The barracks?"

"Ah was helpin' Captain Múdra with something. She's a friend. Was there all night, an' Žofia hadn't made anythin' tae eat yet when Ah left."

Captain Múdra. A friend. Žofia. Another *female* friend.

Anya had a feeling she knew what was going on. Nobles and warriors were all the same. They boasted about all the people they knew and the connections they had. They partied and danced and slept with countless of these *connections.*

Had Anya expected Dmitriy to be any different?

"Do ye want some? It's almost finished." Dmitriy spun the stick between his fingers.

"*Nie,* I don't want to eat a squirrel. I'm going to make some soup. Will you be staying to eat?"

Dmitriy shook his head. "*Nie.* Ah've got tae get back. Ján will be waiting. And Ah have tae visit Masha after that. Ah'll be back..." He grew still for a moment, then added, "Probably tomorrow night."

He was definitely not the sort of person Anya wanted to spend much time around. Not that she was looking for a close friendship or even romance. Life was far too different and the future too unknown for that at the moment. She had also made a point to never get too involved with customers. "Tomorrow night, then. I will have supper ready for you."

"Thank ye, Anya."

"I found a *gusli* in the sitting room. It was under the couch."

"Ah thought Ah heard music when Ah got here."

So he'd been here that long? Anya's cheeks burned. He'd heard her music. Maybe even heard her crying. She would need to be more careful.

Dmitriy stood and limped his way over to a chair, sitting down heavily and massaging his knee with one hand. Anya turned away and started peeling potatoes for the soup. When she looked back up, Dmitriy was staring at the spitted squirrel. As far as she could tell, he hadn't seasoned the meat in any way and was going to it straight out of the flames.

Anya suppressed a shudder.

"I'd like to buy new strings for the *gusli,*" she said a few minutes later. "Is that all right?"

"It's all right."

"Is it yours?"

"Ah suppose so. Came with the house."

"So you knew it was under the couch?"

"Ah think Ah saw it there when Ah looked."

Anya stared at the warrior, who stared right back without blinking. The uneaten squirrel was in his hands, and she realized he still wore the handkerchief across his face. Would he take it off to eat?

"Ye can buy strings if ye want. And ye can have the *gusli.* Ah have nae need for it." Dmitriy stood, tossed the cloak over his shoulder, and tucked the swords into the crook of his arm. "If ye need somethin', Ah'll be at the *hrad.*"

Then he left the kitchen. The disgusting smell of burnt squirrel remained behind.

Chapter 7

Anya Solovyova

Lozveny, the Royal City of Arribor, Second Age, 1998.

The following night came and went with peace and quiet. Anya ate supper with her father, cleaned the dishes, and sat on the front porch to watch the sunset turn the *hrad* golden. She had made cookies earlier, and now she shared them with her father since she had no one else to eat them with.

Anya studied the calluses on her fingers. "I'll probably purchase some *gusli* strings tomorrow. Do you need anything for the garden?"

Father shook his head. "I'm set for now. The roses are blooming well. This earth, Annushka–it's wonderful! The ground is so rich that everything here grows almost without help."

Even the evening air smelled *alive.* Anya closed her eyes and took a deep breath. She could smell the flowers, the dirt, the stone porch beneath her. If she concentrated, she could almost hear voices on the wind, singing with life and laughter from the nearby homes.

Roche was a dead land, where people delighted in slaughter.

Anya opened her eyes. Dmitriy stood in the middle of the garden, his head tilted back so he could stare at the moon. He carried a stack of books in his arms, which looked out of place with his swords.

"We already ate supper," Anya said, annoyed at his unexpected presence. Had he been detained by one of his lady friends? Had he even planned to eat with them in the first place? "But the soup is still warming over the fire."

She should probably get up and prepare him a bowl.

"Are you hungry?"

Dmitriy did not look in her direction. A gust of wind whipped through the garden, carrying a burst of voices and the promise of evening rain.

"Master Vetrov, are you hungry?"

Dmitriy still did not turn. The sun sank beyond the horizon, casting the streets into shadow. Dmitriy nearly faded from sight, wrapped in the darkness.

Anya blinked, and Dmitriy was suddenly standing in front of her, setting the books on the porch. "Ah found these fer ye in the *hrad.* Music books."

Music books! Anya hadn't even considered looking for Arriborn songs and music. She knew most of her own songs by heart and played a lot by ear. But here was an opportunity to learn songs from another land, songs she might never have the privilege of hearing or reading again.

"Music books." Anya placed a hand on the stack. Her fingers itched to touch strings, to try and play something new. Maybe, once she ensured Dmitriy didn't need anything else, she could pull out the *gusli* and try a few songs. "Are you hungry? I can prepare something."

"Ah can eat something."

"Why didn't you answer me earlier?"

Dmitriy's face was unreadable in the shadows. "Ah didnae ken ye were talking tae me. Ah'm sorry."

"That's not your fault," Anya found herself saying. "Come inside. I'll prepare you some supper."

The stack of books was heavy, and Anya nearly dropped them all. Dmitriy took the stack out of her hands and carried it inside. Father followed, picking up the scattered bits of paper that had abandoned the books and tried to escape on the wind.

"Just set them down on the table, and I'll get you something to eat. I have some soup ready. And I made bread this afternoon." Anya recognized her "business" tone in the commands and laughed to herself as she prepared the soup. Treating her employer like he was a guest at her inn—what would she do next? Play a few songs on the *gusli* and ask for coin in return?

Once she'd prepared a bowl, Anya saw about inspecting the books. A few were instructional, teaching the reader how to play various instruments. Her reading skills in the common tongue weren't the best, and she doubted she would bother trying to read them, especially since she already knew how to play.

What really got her excited, though, were the songbooks. She flipped through pages and pages of musical notations, some with notes or lyrics penned alongside. Most were in the common tongue, but one book displayed Rochen writing across the cover.

Anya glanced at Dmitriy, who sat at the table with the untouched bowl of soup at his elbow. "This one is in Rochen."

"Ah ken."

She felt his stare. He knew she was Rochen. Ružena had already explained their circumstances, but she still felt that admitting such a thing in the open would be to risk losing her job. Arriborns did not like Rochen. Roche had started the Red War that had claimed countless lives.

But Dmitriy merely stood and watched her.

Anya flipped the book open and skimmed the first few pages. "These are sacrificial songs," she said with disappointment. "Most are to the Rochen gods for feast days."

There were some songs that Anya chose to never learn or play.

"Ah'm sorry." Dmitriy took the book. "Ah can't read Rochen, or Ah wouldnae brought ye this one." With a casual flick of his wrist, he threw the book into the fireplace.

Anya flinched. "Why would you do that?"

"Those are songs tae a bloodthirsty god who does not exist."

"What if someone finds out? We'll be killed!" Anya reached for the book, but Dmitriy grabbed her arm. "Do you know what happens to someone who destroys anything related to the gods?"

"Ye're in Arribor, Anya. Nae one worships the Rochen gods here. Ah doubt it'll even be missed in the *hrad* library."

"You got it from the *hrad* library? And you burned it?"

Dmitriy nodded.

"You won't be arrested? Pay a fine? Does someone keep track of the books you take out?"

"Nae one keeps track. Take what ye want." Dmitriy returned to the table and poked at the spoon. "Thank ye fer supper. Ah'll eat in mae room."

Anya wondered if she had offended him in some way, then remembered the handkerchief. So he didn't want to take it off in their presence, even to eat? What was he hiding? A scar, perhaps from battle? He was a warrior, after all.

"We're not in Roche anymore." Father stood at the fire and watched the book burn. "I suppose it's hard to forget, when you've lived under the shadow of the priests and their laws for all your life. Old fears and habits are hard to shake off."

Dmitriy wouldn't understand the risk of persecution.

"That was nice of him to bring you these," Father said, pointing towards the books. "Do you think we need to return them to the library when you're finished?"

"I don't know. Probably. Maybe not. I'll ask him." Of course, there was no telling when she might see Dmitriy again. She would take good care of the books and ask about returning them as soon as she could.

"He's certainly kind...when he's home."

Anya glanced in the direction the master of the house had gone, then lowered her voice. "I think he sleeps around."

"Now, there's no reason to assume ill of someone, Annushka, just because they keep odd hours. He's a warrior, isn't he? He must have an important job."

"He said he was helping some captain one night. A *female* captain. And then he mentioned another woman." Anya studied the fire—the songbook was almost nothing but ashes—then cleaned her hands on her apron. "I could be misunderstanding. Or he could just be another noble, living his best life and not worrying about what's right and proper. Either way, what he does is not my business."

"That's true. But it was nice of him to bring you the books. I hope you thanked him."

Anya couldn't remember if she'd thanked him or not.

Father helped her select a few roses from the garden, and she put them on the kitchen table in a brown cup with a quick thank-you note. Her handwriting wasn't the greatest, but at least it was legible.

She spent the evening practicing new songs until her fingertips stung. When she checked in the morning, the flowers and note were gone.

Chapter 8

Anya Solovyova

Ozveny, the Royal City of Arribor, Second Age, 1998.

Days passed, full of quiet monotony. Anya finished cleaning the downstairs and moved on to the upstairs. Besides the two rooms that she and her father slept in and the bedroom at the western end of the house they were not to enter, the house had a fourth bedroom and a small storage room.

If Anya liked to gamble, she would have placed bets that the items in the storage room had been left behind by the previous occupants and Dmitriy had never so much as looked inside the room.

She wasn't going to complain much. Going through the spiderweb-covered boxes and crates gave her something to do and made the days pass quickly. Father finished the front garden and began clearing the old hay and crumbling manure from the small barn. Once the barn was usable, they would see about acquiring chickens and a goat. Anya couldn't wait for fresh goat milk.

Another Sunday came and went. Anya felt more at ease talking to the strangers who approached her after the service. Someone invited her to their house for tea and a prayer meeting with other young women. Father found another gardener and spent a lot of time talking about flowers and seeds.

Anya saw the crowned young man again, sitting in his usual spot. Dmitriy stood behind him like a protective statue. Anya wondered if he was a Christian, or if he only attended the services because the *kráľ* (if it really was the *kráľ*) was a Christian. Or maybe the *kráľ* (if it really was the *kráľ*) only attended because his people expected him to?

She could always ask. But Anya hadn't seen Dmitriy in days, and the thought of asking someone else at the church felt like she was searching for gossip. *Who's that handsome young man with the crown? Is he really a Christian? What about the man standing guard behind him?*

There were better things for her to ponder on Sunday morning–like the sermon.

"Still no news on our second ship," Ružena said after the service. "I'm trying not to worry. But I received a message from Llenned. The ship hasn't even arrived in Stryhaen yet. It could have been delayed leaving Roche."

Anya didn't want to worry either, but worry she did. Had the ship left Roche? Had it sunk between Roche and Llenned? Why hadn't it arrived yet?

And most importantly, was her mother aboard?

"If the ship arrives and Galina is not on it," Father said, "I'm going back to Roche to find her. When do you have people returning?"

"I'm not sure." Ružena bit her lip. "It's been a wet spring. Traveling through the Stryhaen Strait is dangerous when the weather is *good.* I don't know if anyone will risk leaving until these rains let off."

The rain was doing lovely things to the gardens. Anya hadn't considered what it might do to the ocean. She tried not to think about Mother on a tiny ship, tossed about by stormy winds.

It was very hard not to think about it.

Dmitriy came home late that night, but Anya had already gone to bed. She heard someone walking downstairs and imagined thieves and robbers and assassins and enforcers. The noise must have woken her father as well, for she heard him leave his room and take the stairs down to the kitchen.

When he came back upstairs a few minutes later, Anya assumed that meant they were safe. She fell asleep to the smell of roasting meat and groggily resolved to keep something warm in the oven at all hours of the day and night so Dmitriy didn't have to come home and cook his own food.

The idea was a good one. As the days passed, she would wake up to find drying bowls set out on the counter (Dmitriy always washed whatever he used to eat). When Dmitriy made his ghostlike appearances at odd hours of the day, she could prepare a plate for him within a few minutes.

Anya also took to setting things out on the kitchen table with notes for Dmitriy to take care of whenever he was home. Each item she found in the old chests was cleaned and left for Dmitriy to decide what to do with.

Most of the things were clothes, and Dmitriy told her to keep what she wanted and take the rest to Ružena. Ružena said she would deliver them to the deacons at church, who would ensure they found good homes.

But some of the things in the storage room were harder to give away. Old letters. Musty books. A dusty sword that had rusted into its scabbard. Bundles of fabric that were so knotted into mouse nests that their original shape couldn't be identified. Anya did her best to clean them all.

A simple pattern began to fill the weeks. Church services. Shopping. Cooking. Cleaning. Selling things Dmitriy didn't want. Throwing away things that were old and warped beyond use. Practicing on the restrung *gusli* and singing to the growing flowers in the garden. Some days she saw Dmitriy. Some days she saw only signs of his visits. Some days she found no signs at all.

The days grew steadily warmer. Anya spent more and more time outside, staring at the flowers and greenery. Without the ever-present clouds of sacrificial smoke, the air smelled *clean*, and mornings displayed beautiful sunrises. She had heard about the beauty of Arribor, but hearing was nothing compared to seeing the bright skies and colorful gardens.

She would hate to leave it.

"Any news from Roche?" Anya asked Ružena one Sunday afternoon after the service.

"*Nie.* Still nothing about our second ship." Ružena carried a bundle of clothes in her arms—the latest donations from Dmitriy and the storage room. "Your new *kráľ*, Sevastyan, is valiantly fighting for more religious freedom, but it will be a long road." She smiled. "I've learned the Rochen people are stubborn. It's the songs in your blood and bones."

Anya smiled. That was a polite way of putting it. Roche was saturated in hundreds and hundreds of years of bloodshed and idol worship. The priests refused to give up their control and demanded more and more sacrifices in the names of countless gods. Silencers dedicated their lives to Talan and killed for his pleasure. The superstitious were too scared to give up their habits and clung to promises of safety. Many did not see the harm in the bloody beliefs and practices their forefathers walked in.

Kráľ Sevastyan was doing a good thing—trying to lessen the hold the priests had on the people. But he was not a Christian, and his goal was not religious freedom but to bring Roche into the good graces of her neighbors. He dreamed of a green and beautiful land, without the sacrifices and bloodshed that stained her.

Without Christ, changes in Roche would only go so far.

"If I hear any news, I will let you know right away," Ružena promised. "I know you're waiting to hear about your mother."

Anya thought of what Father had said earlier, about returning to Roche. If they received no news of Mother, would he actually return? "When do you think the smugglers will try to go back to Roche?"

"I don't know." Ružena shook her head. "There was an attack in the *hrad* last night. We believe they were trying to kill the *kráľ*.

Three of the assassins were Rochen. We still don't know if they were sent from Roche or only happened to be born there. But if they were operating under Rochen orders, it can't mean things are getting better across the mountains."

The Rochen *kráľ*, Sevastyan Usenko, wouldn't try to assassinate the Arriborn *kráľ*—as far as Anya knew. Sevastyan was working toward peace and trade with Arribor and Llenned. A lot of the Rochen people opposed him. Many thought peace with their neighbors angered the gods and would only bring further anger upon Roche.

If the Arriborn *kráľ* was killed by someone from Roche, even if not under Sevastyan's orders, it could still make peace more difficult. Worst case, it could spark another war. If war broke out, returning to Roche would be impossible. If Mother was still there, she would be unable to join them in Arribor. They would be forever separated.

Anya tried not to think about it as she walked home, but the thought refused to leave her mind: Would she ever see her mother again? If she knew Mother had been discovered and killed, she could find a small measure of peace. Death pulled Christians out of hardships and into the peace and presence of their Savior. But if Mother was still alive, living in hiding, her life would be difficult.

If war broke out, their lives would change yet again. Anya could only thank God that the Arriborn *kráľ* still lived. God had protected him.

Wasn't Dmitriy a bodyguard? Had he been there to protect the *kráľ*? He had stood in his usual place during the church service as if nothing had happened. If Ružena hadn't mentioned it, Anya wouldn't even have known an attack had happened at all.

Dmitriy appeared unharmed. Anya hadn't noticed any signs of him visiting the house recently, so he could have been on duty last night. Or perhaps he had been at some rich woman's house that night, enjoying himself while his *kráľ* was in danger...

Anya shook the thoughts away. Thinking ill of someone was not right. A bodyguard couldn't stand by their charge every moment of the day, and what he did in his time off was not Anya's business. Even if she was his housekeeper.

Once they reached the house, she sat in the garden for a while. Father went inside to take a nap, but Anya doubted she could rest easily. The rainstorms had continued, one afternoon after the other, and Anya was unable to send them away and make the seas calm again. One knife thrust in the dark, and a stranger would lose his life and war might start again. And there was nothing she could do about any of it.

Back home, she had always been able to do something. If Mother needed help in the kitchen, she could peel potatoes. If the inn was full of customers, she could take orders, bring drinks, or play music to entertain them. If chores needed done, she could do them.

Here, she was powerless. Useless. The only thing she could do was continue cleaning Dmitriy's house as if nothing had happened. She could poke through the next chest of abandoned clothes, cook meals only she and Father would eat, and haggle over the price of flour with the closest seller in the market square.

And then someday, suddenly, she would hear news about war with Roche. She would be stuck in Arribor for the rest of her life. Right now, as she sat in the warm sunshine with flowers surrounding her, that fate didn't sound too bad. But when she thought about Mother, about the home and business they had worked so hard to grow, about everything she had left behind, the possibility chilled her to the bone.

Tea. That was what she needed. A warm cup of tea and maybe something to eat. Then she could return to the garden and bring all her thoughts and fears to God.

She smelled blood the moment she stepped into the house. It brought back memories of sacrificial days, of walking past silencer arenas, of watching her sister die in front of a cheering crowd. Anya swallowed. Had something happened to Father? Maybe the assassins had failed at killing the *krâl'* and had come to kill any Rochen Christians they found in Arribor. *That* would surely please their gods—killing those who tried to escape.

Anya hesitated at the foot of the stairs. Was Father upstairs? Where was the smell of blood coming from? What if the assassins were still in the house? Should she run for help? Who would help them?

Something clattered in the kitchen, and Anya left the stairs, tiptoeing through the hallway and peeking around the doorframe. A man sat before the fire, wrapping a bandage around his arm. Dark hair was twisted into a tail at the back of his head, and his clean-shaven face was covered in black silencer tattoos.

Anya froze. Silencers were rarely seen outside the arenas. When they were released, it was under the instructions of their masters with a guard force to ensure they returned to captivity. They only left the games to spill blood elsewhere. No one freed silencers. They were raised to do one thing: kill.

If a silencer was in Arribor, he must have been sent by his master to kill someone. There had been an attack on the *kráľ* last night.

And now the house smelled like blood.

Chapter 9

Anya Solovyova

Ozveny, the Royal City of Arribor, Second Age, 1998.

Anya turned and fled. She tripped twice on her way up the stairs, banging her shins on the hard wood. The taste of blood filled her mouth, and she nearly gagged. Father's bedroom door was closed. She opened it without knocking, images of him lying dead on the floor filling her mind. At least silencers were quick. He wouldn't suffer.

Father lay on his back on top of the blankets, an arm over his eyes. He sat up as Anya raced inside. "Is something wrong?"

"There's a silencer in the kitchen. We need to leave." Anya wasn't sure if she was whispering or shouting. The words came fast, and she couldn't stop them. "Someone tried to kill the *kráľ*, and now he's downstairs. I thought you were dead. We need to get out of here! We need to go back to Roche!"

"Anya, calm down. What's happened?" Father swung his feet over the side of the bed and stood. "Take a breath."

"We have to leave!" Anya grabbed Father's hand and pulled him toward the door. She tripped on his shoes that he'd left on the floor by the bed. They had no time to grab anything. It was like the raid of their inn all over again.

People screaming. Men with swords. The smell of blood.

She was too late. The silencer stood in the doorway, covered in shadows. Anya had never witnessed the horrors of the arenas, but she had seen enough public killings to know how quick a well-trained silencer could be. They only needed a few seconds, and they never showed mercy.

Silencers didn't even know what mercy *was.*

There had been no mercy when her sister had been killed. No hesitation. A sword had pierced her heart in a single thrust.

"Is everything all right?" the silencer asked. His accent wasn't Rochen. He took a step into the room, into the light from the open window. Anya recognized Dmitriy by his dark eyes and the dip in his shoulder when he walked.

Dmitriy was a silencer. Not only did he bear a Rochen slave tattoo on his jaw, but marks from silencer arenas dotted his cheeks, declaring feats and wins. Anya couldn't remember what each one meant, but he had *many.*

Dmitriy was a *good* silencer. Which meant they were going to die.

"Don't come any closer!" Father stepped in front of Anya and held out a hand. "You have no reason to kill us."

Father could do nothing against a silencer. Even if Dmitriy didn't have his swords, he could make a kill. The silencer who'd killed Vera had used a sword. Anya wouldn't even die the same way as her sister.

"Artyom, Anya. Ah'm not going tae hurt ye." Dmitriy held out his hands. "Please."

"You're a silencer! You kill Christians. You're a murderer." Anya pointed a finger. "That's why you wear the handkerchief. You've been hiding it. Someone sent you to assassinate the *král'*, and you almost succeeded last night!"

Father clenched his fists. "Please, let us go. Have mercy."

Silencers didn't know mercy.

Anya clasped her hands. Dmitriy had been kind to them. He'd brought her music books, thanked her for cooking, and listened to her music with polite attention. He'd studied the flowers in the garden and seemed to enjoy the changes Father had made.

He had become a friend, or almost a friend. Had it all been a lie? "Please, *please*, let us go." Whether she was asking Dmitriy or praying to God, she wasn't sure. Maybe both.

Dmitriy took a step back, then another. The shadows of the hallway seemed to grow, wrapping him in darkness and pulling him out of view. "Okay," he said, his voice barely a whisper. "Ah won't hurt ye."

Anya didn't hear him leave. She knew she wouldn't hear a single step he took. She never did. When Rochen soldiers had visited the inn, they'd jingled with buckles and spurs. Dmitriy was always silent.

"We're leaving," Father said. He grabbed his boots from beside the bed and pulled them on. "Now!"

They passed through the hallway, down the stairs, and out the front door. Anya picked up speed through the garden and was in a full run by the time they reached the street.

She ran as fast as she could, putting distance between her and the silencer with every step. Tears stung her eyes and burned her cheeks. Her lungs ached. Her father slowed, but still she ran. No matter how hard she tried to forget, the memory of a silencer's sword cutting through Vera's heart chased her on.

Chapter 10

Anya Solovyova

Ozveny, the Royal City of Arribor, Second Age, 1998.

"Anya! What happened?" Ružena wiped Anya's face with a flour-coated apron. "You look like you've been chased halfway across the city!"

Anya stumbled into Ružena's dining room and collapsed into a chair. Father sat down heavily beside her, his breath rattling in his throat. For a moment, neither of them spoke.

"Dmitriy's a silencer," Anya said at last. "Why didn't you tell us? Or did you not know?"

If Ružena didn't know, maybe the *kráľ* didn't know. Maybe Dmitriy was in Arribor to spy for Roche. Maybe his master was planning to kill the *kráľ*.

"I knew," Ružena said.

Anya buried her head in her hands. "Then why did you let us live there? Why didn't you tell us?"

"Because I trust Dmitriy. You are safe with him, I can promise you that."

"Even though he's a silencer?"

"He's not a silencer anymore."

That was impossible. Freedom from slavery didn't exist in Roche. Once a slave mark was tattooed on your face, you were a slave for the rest of your life. Sometimes slaves escaped on ships and sailed to lands where they could be free. But silencers? They lived in heavily guarded arenas. They knew nothing about the world beyond the games.

"I see you don't believe me." Ružena turned toward the kitchen. "Come and help me finish my *pirohy*. I will tell you everything I know about Dmitriy. I promise you—he is safe."

Anya did not budge. "My sister was killed by a silencer. She knelt in the street, and he killed her in one blow." The memory brought fresh tears to Anya's eyes. She sniffed, afraid she wouldn't be able to finish speaking. "And the people cheered as she died."

Ružena said nothing.

"I can't go back," Anya continued. "I'm sorry. I can't. Even if you say he's not like that. You're not from Roche. You don't know what silencers can do."

"*Nie.*" Ružena shook her head. "I don't. I've never been across the mountains, but I do know what Dmitriy is capable of. Many of my friends and family are alive today because of his bravery. I trust him with their lives—and with yours."

Father found his breath again. "He's a silencer. They are raised from birth to do nothing but kill."

"I thought, as Christians, you would be able to look beyond someone's past. You should know what God's grace can do in a heart." Ružena's tone was kind. "But I won't ask you to go back. You both may stay here until we find a different place."

"There is no need. We will return to Roche with the next group of smugglers."

"To where all the silencers are?" Ružena raised an eyebrow. "Might be dangerous."

Anya could forgive Ružena for not understanding how dangerous silencers were. But to joke about it? How could Ružena laugh about their fear when Anya had seen the work of silencers with her own eyes? Ružena had not lived in the shadow of the arenas all her life. Ružena had not smelled blood and death when the wind blew the right way.

"Silencers are murderers. Killers." Anya closed her eyes, forcing away memories. "Everyone in Roche knows that. I cannot live with or work for a silencer." Even if a silencer was thought to be *safe*, he still had blood on his hands. He still had a lifetime of death behind him.

"And you don't believe someone can repent of that? You don't think someone who was once a murderer can become a Christian?" Ružena pointed a flour-covered finger at Anya. "Do you think God is unable to save a silencer?"

Dmitriy was a Christian? Anya wouldn't have guessed. He attended the church services but stood behind the *kráľ* like a guard. He hadn't ever mentioned God to Anya. He didn't even pray before he ate.

Not that Anya had ever seen him eat, now that she thought about it. He always took food into his room, or else came and went when no one was in the house.

"Christ died for the worst of sinners," Anya said at last. "I believe that. He can save silencers."

"And I have confidence that Dmitriy is a Christian."

"But I can't go back. I won't be able to look at him, Ružena. Even if he wears that handkerchief, I *know* what's underneath." Anya glanced at Father. "I have nightmares now, nightmares of my sister. I won't be able to sleep knowing there might be a silencer at the far end of the hall, or downstairs in the kitchen."

Ružena hesitated. "I understand your fears. But I assure you, Dmitriy is—"

Father interrupted, his voice gentle. "I'm sure you are correct, Lady Ružena. He has been good to us. I'm certain he is as trustworthy as you say. But the death of my daughter at the hands of a silencer is still too fresh."

Anya nodded.

"Please, offer him our apologies. It is not his fault. And put us to work while we remain in your house. You let us stay as guests once before. I would hate to continue living off your kindness."

"If you are settled, I will see what I can do." Ružena did not look pleased. "But I still think you are passing up the best situation possible. It will be difficult to find another."

"I understand." Anya took a deep breath. "We're grateful for your help. And it's only temporary. I suppose we're going home soon."

The prospect of returning to Roche did not excite her as much as she thought.

Chapter 11

Anya Solovyova

Lozveny, the Royal City of Arribor, Second Age, 1998.

It didn't take Anya long to decide that she was born to work in a bakery. Taking orders and packaging purchases was easy and reminded her of working at the *Quiet Waters* with her family. She enjoyed greeting the customers and making sure they got what they needed. The constant smell of fresh bread and cookies was an additional delight.

"You'll get tired of the smell and the constant traffic." Yekaterina leaned against the counter and watched Anya count out change for a customer. "There's never any time to sit down."

Anya wiped her hands on her apron. "That only makes the day go by faster. Now, when the bread on the counter is all sold, do we need to make more?"

"There's more in the back." Yekaterina yawned. "But I don't bother bringing it out. The customers all know what they want, anyway. I just wait until they come in and ask for it."

"But are we supposed to keep the counter display full?"

"It's not *that* important."

Anya had known Yekaterina for years and liked to think she could call her a friend. The girl's family had often attended the secret worship services at *Quiet Waters,* and while Anya and Yekaterina lived very different lives, they both shared a secret that could get them killed–their faith in God.

But Anya hadn't realized how spoiled and unused to work Yekaterina was until now. Apparently, the past few weeks of working a job had done little to change Yekaterina's attitude. She still stared at people as if they were beneath her and gave them their purchases like a master handing out tasks to a servant. Her hair was braided and covered with a beaded cap as if she was going to a party. Anya wondered where the cap had come from. Had someone put it in the clothing donations? Or had Yekaterina purchased it as soon as she'd earned enough money?

Anya glanced at the door, almost expecting it to burst open with another horde of customers. "I'm going to get more bread. If things are out for people to see, they might be interested and buy more."

"Oh. I suppose so." Yekaterina made no move to help but continued to lean on the counter while Anya brought out different loaves to arrange in a tidy display. The owner of the bakery, a woman named Lujza, kept a good supply of items in the back, though Anya noted that a few shelves were running low.

"When will Lujza be back? Do we need to pull the bread out of the oven soon?"

"I don't know." Yekaterina shrugged. "She comes and goes. But she always takes the bread out. You don't need to worry about it."

"Did she ask you to watch the bread?"

"When I first started here, she asked me to take it out. But I burnt myself. I'm not a baker, so I said I wouldn't do it again. I'm good at other things."

Anya wasn't surprised that the owner didn't trust Yekaterina with the baking. "What *are* you good at?"

"I play the *gusli.* I can paint. I'm very good at painting." Yekaterina pointed to a plate of cookies. "See the shapes? I'm good at shaping the cookies too."

Now that Anya examined the cookies, she could see they took the shapes of cats and dogs and flowers. "Those are nice."

Yekaterina beamed. "The children love them!"

Anya forgave the noble girl. Maybe Yekaterina merely needed a little more time to adjust to working for her living.

The door to the bakery opened, and two women trailed by an entire group of children barged in. Anya smiled and greeted them, and Yekaterina stood and held out the plate of cookies. "Hello!"

The children eagerly helped themselves to the cookies, arguing over which ones they wanted and even putting back the ones that broke in half. Yekaterina laughed and teased them, but she also made sure the shyest child received a whole, untouched cookie for himself.

The women asked for their bread orders, and Anya went into the back to find them. Reading the handwriting took her a moment, but she found the bread that had been baked earlier that day and brought out the parcels. During the time she was in the back, the women had apparently seen a few things on the display counter and had added them to their purchases.

Anya snuck a glance at Yekaterina, but she did not notice.

"I heard the Nobility Council is trying to remove that Crown Warrior again," the woman with flowers in her braided hair said. "There's a meeting tomorrow."

"Again? Even after last night? He protected the *kráľ*." The other woman held a small baby in her arms and clutched it a little tighter as she spoke. "They said it was a Rochen attack."

Anya supposed her accent wasn't noticeable. Or perhaps these women didn't mind being served by a Rochen.

"I think that's why it was brought up again. Dmitriy Vetrov fades into the shadows and people forget about him." Flower-Braids laughed. "Then something like this happens, and everyone remembers his slaughter of the North Band."

The bread was all packaged, and Anya was ready for payment. The conversation might have ended there. But Yekaterina, with eyes wide as an owl, said, "What slaughter?"

"You don't remember the murder of Ivan Kostra and the slaughter of the North Band?" Flower-Braids fixed a glare on

Yekaterina. "My husband served under Ivan Kostra. He witnessed Dmitriy Vetrov cut his way through an entire hallway of North Band warriors. He saw the Captain-General lying dead in that demon's wake."

Crown Warrior. Dmitriy Vetrov. Anya remembered the flash of a silencer's sword and the smell of blood. The person this woman spoke of had to be Dmitriy. Who else was a protector of the *král*? Who else could be capable of such a slaughter?

"My husband says that Vetrov was only left alive because he fought against Ivan Kostra to protect the royal family. But the people of Ozveny haven't forgotten. The dead of the North Band were more Arriborn than the tainted Drobný line." Flower-Braids handed Anya the money for her bread. "The war brought much death to our land. If we had surrendered to Roche, perhaps our loved ones would still be alive right now."

Anya counted the money, thanked the woman, then turned to the other. "Do you need anything else?"

The woman with the baby shook her head. "*Nie.* That's all."

Once the little group was gone and the bakery was quiet again, Anya turned to Yekaterina. "I forgot to ask how much you sell those cookies for."

"Oh, I don't sell them. I give them out." Yekaterina set the plate down and poked a finger at the crumbs. "Do they really think Arribor should have surrendered?"

"Apparently." Anya wondered if Dmitriy had really killed an entire band of warriors, if the Arriborn people truly thought their lives would have been better under Roche, and if Lujza knew that Yekaterina was giving away free cookies.

"If Arribor surrendered, this place would soon look like home." Yekaterina twirled a finger in the cookie crumbs. "Sacrificial smoke would fill the air. Christians would go into hiding. The priests would build idols on every corner. Life was hard in Roche, but I didn't realize how bad it was until I came here."

"Arriborns don't understand what it's truly like in Roche," Anya agreed. "They don't know what it's like to live in fear all of one's life."

Arriborns didn't understand that a lifetime spent fearing silencers couldn't be erased with a single affirmation of someone's intentions. Anya had every reason to fear Dmitriy. At least she wouldn't need to see him again.

In a few more days, she would be heading home. The group of smugglers was planning to return to Roche over the mountains. Father and Anya would go with them. Her time in Arribor was coming to an end.

Lujza returned shortly afterward, and Anya was glad for the distraction. Even Yekaterina seemed excited and detached herself from the counter to follow Lujza around and tell her about all the different customers that had visited the store.

Anya helped pull the bread out of the great ovens, learned how to prepare for the orders that would be expected tomorrow, and watched Yekaterina shape another batch of cookies. The noble girl was talented—that much was certain. If she found motivation to work a little harder, she could do quite well in the bakery business.

Anya was a little disappointed that she wouldn't be around to see it. Maybe she could write to Yekaterina, and they could share news. That would be nice.

The walk from the bakery back to Ružena's house was long and almost entirely uphill. Why the Arriborns had decided to build their capital city on the top of a great rise in the middle of nowhere was a mystery. There was probably some reasoning behind it—a better view, or protection against enemies, perhaps. But it certainly made travel through the streets difficult.

She was out of breath and sweating by the time she reached the house, but the money in her pocket and the confidence from a successful day of work made everything worth it.

Supper was ready when Anya entered the kitchen. Father must have helped, because the beet salad smelled similar to the salad he used to make back at home. And indeed, he was setting out plates when Anya peeked into the dining room. "I hope you're hungry, Annushka!"

Even though she had smelled bread and sugar all day, Anya was hungry. She stepped into the dining room, prepared to collapse into a chair, and saw a familiar *gusli* propped up in a seat, like it had been invited to supper.

"How'd that get here?" Anya demanded. She bent to inspect it, checking the strings and the fretboard. Sure enough, it was Dmitriy's *gusli*.

"Dmitriy stopped by this afternoon and returned our things. He asked that you keep the *gusli*, saying he didn't need it."

Of course. A silencer would have no need for a *gusli.* He wouldn't know how to play it. Dmitriy was hardly ever home. He was too busy spending time with women and terrifying the people of Ozveny.

"I don't want it." The words tumbled from Anya's lips. "He shouldn't have bothered."

Father said nothing. He picked up the *gusli* and moved it into a corner of the room. "I would do something with it, then. Ružena has been out all afternoon and doesn't know it's here. I have a feeling she would want you to keep it."

Of course Ružena would want Anya to keep it. And perhaps there was no harm in keeping the instrument. Anya would think about it overnight, and if she still couldn't stand the sight of it in the morning, she would return it. She didn't want anything from a murderer.

CHAPTER 12

ANYA SOLOVYOVA

LOZVENY, THE ROYAL CITY OF ARRIBOR, SECOND AGE, 1998.

Anya still hated the sight of the *gusli* in the morning. She stared at it as she dressed and brushed her hair and tried to forget about it while she prayed. But the more she thought about it, the more annoyed she became.

She didn't need a *gusli.* She was going home in a few weeks, and she certainly didn't want to take an instrument with her across the mountains. It was too nice of a thing to risk damaging just because she didn't want to buy another one once she reached Roche.

If she kept the *gusli,* Ružena would probably urge her to take it anyway, and Anya would have to admit her chief reason for not wanting to keep the instrument: every time she looked at it, she was reminded of the silencer it belonged to.

She was going to take it back.

"I'm heading out early," she told her father as she breezed through the kitchen with the *gusli* on her back. "I'm going to return this, then head to work. I'll eat something at the bakery."

"Be safe," he called before turning back to his breakfast.

If Anya's guess was correct, Dmitriy's house would be empty. He came and went at the oddest hours but was always gone in the mornings. She had never once seen him at breakfast. If he was home in the evening, he was up early and gone before she woke.

She had plenty of time to slip into the kitchen and leave the *gusli*. She might have to run to reach the bakery in time, but at least it would be mostly downhill. The morning was still cool, and the weather was nice. She would enjoy a good run.

As she expected, the house was dark and empty. Orange ashes glowed in the fire–the only sign Dmitriy had been home recently. He must have eaten something for supper, which meant he was probably out by now.

Anya's plan had been to leave the *gusli* on the kitchen table and flee the house, but she had a feeling it would be left there for a long time. It was too precious an instrument to sit on a table and risk getting knocked off or carried around improperly.

She decided to leave it in the sitting room, back under the couch where she'd found it. It would be safe from harm there. She sat on the floor and loosened the strings, resisting the urge to play one final tune. This was not the time for music.

"Goodbye," she said, tucking the instrument under the couch on a bed of blankets.

Now all she had to do was leave.

Except it felt wrong to leave the *gusli* without letting Dmitriy know it was there. He might never go in the sitting room, and even if he did, he might not notice the instrument. Anya should probably leave him a note.

She ransacked the kitchen and found nothing she could use for leaving a message. She went to her old room and was halfway up the steps before she remembered that he'd taken all her things to Ružena's house.

Well, she would have to tell Ružena after all. Ružena could pass the message on to Dmitriy once Anya and her father were on their way to Roche. The *gusli* would be fine, but now Anya would have to admit to Ružena that she'd returned the gift.

The door to Dmitriy's study caught Anya's eye at the bottom of the stairs. There would surely be paper in there. While she had worked here, Anya had carefully obeyed his wish to stay out of the study and his bedroom.

She saw nothing wrong with requesting privacy, but now Anya wondered–what was he hiding? Rochen spies? Dead bodies? She didn't *want* to see dead bodies, but this would be her only chance to find out.

If she discovered something suspicious, she would find one of those warriors that patrolled the city streets. She would turn Dmitriy in as a spy and a murderer. The Council that hated him so much would have her willing voice to testify.

If there was nothing out of the ordinary? Then Anya would leave Dmitriy alone. She would return to Roche and never think of him again. If he was truly a Christian or not was between Dmitriy and God. It wasn't like she had planned to marry him or anything.

Anya pushed the study door open. The one window was covered with a dark cloak, blocking out most of the sun. It also kept people outside from looking in (as Anya had discovered early on in her job). The dim light through the fabric and the firelight from the open door was just enough to see by.

Wooden crates lined one wall, opposite a small desk. She saw no fireplace, no chairs, no signs of comfort or even frequent use. Anya opened the desk drawers and found neat stacks of clean paper inside but nothing to write with. The top of the desk only displayed a map, spread out and held down with a small knife.

Well, her lawbreaking seemed quite pointless. She still didn't have writing utensils for a note, and there was nothing inside that she deemed worth hiding. If anything, she should have been allowed to enter this room at will and include it in her cleaning. It wasn't as dusty as the completely unused rooms, but a good sweeping and airing-out were needed.

Maybe she should try his bedroom? Anya shook her head. She'd already broken his rules to check the study. She would leave his bedroom alone. If he didn't have writing materials in the study, why would he have them in his bedroom?

Leaving a message with Ružena would have to suffice.

Anya turned away from the desk. Dmitriy stood in the doorway, clad in his handkerchief, cloak, and swords. It was such a familiar sight that a moment passed before Anya found her terror.

Dmitriy, her employer.

Dmitriy, the silencer.

Dmitriy, her employer, who was a silencer, who had also told her not to go into the very room she was currently standing in.

"I was looking for something to write with," Anya squeaked. "I'm returning the *gusli.* Your study needs cleaning. Why do you have a cloak over the window? You should buy some curtains."

She knew she was rambling. She knew she should be on her knees, asking for forgiveness and begging for her life. But Dmitriy continued to stare, and each moment spent standing meant she had another moment to live. And as long as she was alive, she was going to talk.

"It's a nice little study. The window would open into the gardens and let in the smell of the flowers, if you allowed it. Why do you close it off?"

Dmitriy turned and walked away, approaching the kitchen table. With his back to Anya, he unbuckled the large sword he carried on his shoulders.

She was going to die. Might as well make it worth it. "Ružena said you were a Christian. I guess she was wrong."

Dmitriy set the big sword on the table, then drew the two swords from his belt. Anya wondered if that meant he was going to kill her slowly, cutting her life away bit by bit instead of with one great thrust.

"My sister was killed by a silencer because she didn't worship the Rochen gods. I'm not afraid to die."

"Ah'm not goin' tae kill ye." Dmitriy set the two swords on the table as well, then placed a few knives with the other weapons. When he turned to face Anya, he held his empty hands out. "Ah just want tae talk."

Anya backed toward the desk and grabbed the knife that had been laid on the map. "Don't come any closer!"

"Ah understand ye donnae want tae stay here."

"I'm not working for a silencer."

Dmitriy said nothing. Anya wondered if he had taken that as an insult. Had she meant it as an insult? She wasn't sure. "My sister was killed by one," she added. "I know it wasn't your doing. But I don't want to think about it every time I see you."

"Then Ah'll keep this on." Dmitriy gestured to the handkerchief on his face.

"Thank you." Anya adjusted her grip on the knife. She knew he could easily overpower her and take the weapon away, but she would make it as difficult for him as she could.

"Why did ye come back?"

"I was returning the *gusli*."

"Ye donnae want it?"

He definitely sounded offended now. "I'm leaving soon, and I won't need it." Anya waited for him to ask about her trespassing, about her presence in the forbidden study, about her leaving her job.

"Yer going with the *Biblia* smugglers? Back tae Roche?"

Anya nodded. "How did you know?"

"Ružena told me." Dmitriy gestured to the boxes against the wall. "Those are some of the *Biblias.* Ah'm storin' them fer Múdra."

Múdra. That was one of the names he'd mentioned before. "Who's that?"

"She's the Captain of the West Band. Ah dae patrols fer her, when warriors are out sick. An' she helps the smugglers as well."

So this Múdra was not a lover of some kind? Anya knew she had formed her own opinion without much evidence, but how could she have guessed that Dmitriy worked with the *Biblia* smugglers?

"Ah ken ye think Ah'm a murderer. An' yer right, Ah killed in the silencer arenas." Dmitriy bowed his head. "Ah'm a Christian now, but Ah still carry mae sword tae defend Ján. Ah understand why ye donnae want tae stay here. But Ah want ye tae ken..."

He went silent for a long time, and Anya finally lowered the knife. "Understand what?"

"That yer safe here."

Something in his words twisted her stomach. A silencer killed. A silencer did not provide *safety.* Yet there was something in Dmitriy's tone, a quiet confidence that made Anya believe he meant it.

Dmitriy had only ever been kind to her. She was used to crude comments from customers, and even worse ones from the sailors that had filled the streets around the inn. She'd had to turn down even well-intentioned patrons and neighbors if they'd showed interest. As soon as they discovered she was a Christian, it would all be over, and her life would be at risk.

Anya was the one who had assumed ill of Dmitriy's character. She had been the one to call him a murderer. Even after he'd offered her a job and a place to stay, brought her books from the *hrad,* and tried to make sure she felt safe despite breaking one of his requests, she still feared him.

She needed to make this right.

"I'm sorry I came into your study. I should not have." Anya set the knife back on the desk. "Please forgive me."

Dmitriy continued to sit on the floor and tilted his head as Anya walked closer. From their positions, she could have kicked him soundly in the jaw. She'd seen Christians treated in such ways before.

"How does a silencer become a Christian?" she asked, putting her hands on her hips. "And how did you come to Arribor?"

"The war."

Anya waited. Dmitriy did not offer to explain further.

"How did you hear the Gospel?" Anya tried again.

"Mae friend Duren told me. Ee said that Talan wasn't real."

Talan, the Rochen god of the silencers. Anya knew the name. No one but the silencers worshipped him. They sang to him before the games, asking for success, but the only sacrifices they offered were their own blood.

Silencers who killed their masters would be punished eternally, as far as she remembered. It was one way of keeping trained killers in line.

"Ah feared Talan, like all silencers. But Duren...ee was right. Talan is not real. And Duren's God died for us, even the murderers. Isn't that somethin'?"

A Christian silencer. In her heart, Anya knew she believed such a thing could exist. The Gospel reached all sorts of sinners. But how could a silencer learn about the true God in the confinement and isolation of the arenas? Why had she never considered that they, too, needed salvation?

"I'm glad," Anya said at last. "I think, if I had the time, I should hear your story. But I need to get to work."

"Lujza's bakery."

"You know?" A bit of unease crept down her spine. "How?"

"Lujza told me. She spars with Captain Múdra."

"Does everyone in Ozveny know each other?"

Dmitriy's voice held a hint of amusement. "Múdra knows almost everyone. And her West Band warriors keep an eye on the rest. Nothing happens in Ozveny that she doesn't learn about."

Anya was probably long overdue for a meeting with this person.

"Ah can walk ye tae Lujza's. Ah 'ave nothing tae dae today."

"You're not working?"

"Not right now. Ján sent me away. The Council has more complaints."

Anya had heard something about that. "The North Band?"

Dmitriy stood and slid a finger under his handkerchief, adjusting it. "They forget that Ah left many of the North Band warriors alive. But they won't forget that Ah won."

Anya had no place scorning the Nobility Council for their easy loss of memory. Hadn't she seen nothing but a murderer when she'd looked at him?

Even now, the prospect of him walking her to the bakery made her uneasy. The time spent marching through the streets would be the perfect opportunity to think over the conversation they'd just had. She had all sorts of things to work out—embarrassment over getting caught in his house, shame at running from him when she'd first learned what he had been.

But when Dmitriy opened the kitchen door and let in the smell of wet stone and the patter of raindrops, Anya accepted his offer of a spare cloak and a guiding hand into the storm.

Chapter 13

Anya Solovyova

Lozveny, the Royal City of Arribor, Second Age, 1998.

The door to the bakery was stuck, and Dmitriy had to wiggle it open. It scraped the stone underneath, alerting everyone in the store to Anya's arrival. She pushed back the dripping hood of Dmitriy's extra cloak and met Lujza's surprised glance.

"Late on your second day of work." Lujza raised an eyebrow.

"It's mae fault, Lujza." Dmitriy bowed. "Ah kept her at mae house fer a bit."

Yekaterina spit out the cookie she was eating, spewing crumbs across the counter.

"You really don't want to phrase it like that, Dmitriy." Lujza shook her head. "What were you doing?"

"She threatened mae with a knife an' Ah told her Ah was a silencer an' that she's safe." Dmitriy moved to the corner of the shop and inspected a shelf of freshly baked loaves. "She was returnin' that *gusli.* Ján sent me home tae wait out the Council. And Ah told 'er Ah'd walk 'er here."

He set a loaf on the counter and flicked a coin out from the folds of his cloak. "So don't blame Anya. It's mae fault. Do ye have cheese in the back?"

"You've spent too much time with Duren if you think you can ask me for food like you're ordering in a tavern." Lujza moved to the doorway leading to the back of the store. "Don't just stand there, Anya. Go hang up that cloak and get to work. I have fresh-baked cookies that need to go up to the *hrad.*"

Anya slid off the cloak and hung it on the wall with another cloak that must have been Lujza's. Yekaterina appeared far too damp to have walked outside with one on.

"Thank you, Dmitriy," she said once Lujza was gone. "You didn't have to do that."

"Mae fault. Ah should have let ye leave."

Anya took his coin and pushed the bread across the counter. "I'm sure Lujza will let you eat in the back, if you need some privacy."

"Ah'll be fine. Lujza kens." Dmitriy tilted his head toward Yekaterina. "Will she be all right?"

Yekaterina was still watching Dmitriy with wide eyes.

"I don't know," Anya said.

Lujza returned with a few slices of cheese on a plate. "Go sit down and eat. And if you have nothing to do afterward, I have a few errands you can run."

Dmitriy took the plate, set the bread on it, and moved to the darkest corner of the room. He unbuckled his great sword and leaned it against his shoulder as he sat. After a quick glance at Anya and Yekaterina, he slid the handkerchief down from his face and began to eat.

Anya turned away. Even if Dmitriy wasn't going to attack, even if he was *safe*, she still didn't want to see his tattoos. Now was not the time to wonder what each mark meant or to ponder how skilled he might have been in the arena.

"Anya, can you come help me prepare the orders?" Lujza asked. "Yekaterina, keep an eye on the store, please. And don't stare at Dmitriy. That's not polite."

Yekaterina fixed her owl eyes on Lujza. "Is he...?"

"Crown Warrior to the *kráľ*? *Áno.* Let him eat in peace while he's off duty." Lujza pulled Anya into the back room. "You remember my method for packing cookies?"

Anya remembered and was soon busy working. Lujza had horrible handwriting, and deciphering the orders was the hardest part. If she had to deliver them, her job would be almost impossible—even if she could read the street names, she would have no idea where to go. Thankfully, finding the baked goods and wrapping them in baskets was all she had to do.

Not sampling the goods required all her self-control. Back home, she used to drop into the kitchen and help herself to whatever her mother or Vera were making. With customers that came at all hours of the day, there was always something hot and ready and tasty.

When they finished preparing the orders, Lujza took two of the baskets to Dmitriy. "Can you deliver this to Eliška Poduska? And then this one goes to the Inland Band barracks."

"The Poduskas, then the Inland Band," Dmitriy repeated. "Understood."

"Thank you, Dmitriy. I appreciate the help." Lujza waved at Yekaterina. "You come with me. My delivery girl is sick today, and I'll need help carrying all these without getting them wet. Anya, can she take your cloak?"

"It's actually Dmitriy's."

"Dmitriy, can she take your cloak?"

"*Áno.*"

A minute later, the bakery was quiet and empty. Anya stood behind the counter and stared at the puddles left from the dripping cloaks. She would need to find something to clean those up. And Dmitriy had left his empty plate in the corner. That needed to be put away as well. But when the door opened and her first customer walked in, cleaning was quickly put out of her mind.

Mornings were busy, judging by her only two days at work. People wanted their items hot and fresh, and Anya couldn't blame them. Lujza had a gift for baking.

Customers came and went, and Anya embraced the business. She'd mull over the events of the morning later. Quick conversations, counting money, and wrapping bread soon stole all her attention. One greeting, one smile, and one farewell came right after another.

"It's about time we met," one woman said, changing a standard encounter into something that shattered Anya's usual reply.

The woman was short and dressed in the familiar blue *rubhaka* that Anya had seen many of the Arriborn warriors wear. The sword at her side and dripping cloak only made her occupation more obvious.

"Can I help you?" Anya asked.

"Here to pick up an order. I'm Captain Múdra."

Captain Múdra. The woman Dmitriy had mentioned, the one who helped him store *Biblias* for the smugglers. As Anya went to the back to retrieve the order, she wondered if she should say something. Would it be strange to mention their connections? Did Captain Múdra even have time for light conversation?

She would ask. It was only polite. And she might never have another chance to talk to the woman.

"I heard you were helping Lujza around here. Dmitriy had high praise for you. With a recommendation like that, we knew you'd work well at the bakery."

"Dmitriy told you about me?" Anya set the package down. The thought of Dmitriy talking to other people about her was rather strange.

"Well, I haggled it out of him. But he said you were always busy, and his house was like a different place. He also said you play the *gusli.*" Captain Múdra leaned on the counter. "If you are interested, my warriors gather in the barracks twice a week to play and sing. Anyone is invited, and it's a lot of fun."

"Where are your barracks? And when is the next gathering?" Anya didn't have an instrument, but maybe she could attend and listen. She still had a few days left in Arribor.

"There's one tonight at the West Band barracks. Come up to the *hrad* and ask anyone you see. They'll help you get there." Múdra did not move. "Also, if you're interested, the Nobility Council has recently created a new position in the *hrad.* They're seeking some sort of Master of Music, or whatever they're calling it."

"Sounds important."

"Maybe. Apparently, they want someone in charge of the music at all their events. There are lots of parties and dances and silly things, and they usually take turns finding minstrels or bards. Some recent complaints about the music has them on the lookout for someone to handle that for them."

"I would say that's important, then. Especially for a dance. You can't just take the first *gusli* player you find on the streets and expect them to play decent music."

Múdra beamed. "I knew you would understand! Unfortunately, the Council offered to grant one request to whoever earns the title, and now everyone who can hold a lute is going to audition. It will be a disaster!"

Anya could only imagine. Many minstrels had passed through *Quiet Waters.* Some she let play on their own and earn their supper by entertaining the guests. Sometimes she even joined them, sharing songs and music. Others were so bad that she had to ask them to put their instruments away for fear of chasing away paying customers.

"You should audition. It would pay quite well. Much better than working in a bakery."

"I don't have an instrument, and I'm leaving in a few days. Back to Roche."

"Oy, that's right!" Múdra shook her head. "I heard you and your father were going back with Šimon's group. Pity. You've been quite a blessing to some of my dear friends. I pray you will be safe in your return home."

"Thank you."

Múdra took the wrapped purchase and turned to leave. Her head tilted toward the corner of the room where Dmitriy had eaten, and she paused. "Dmitriy has been here, hasn't he?"

"How did you know?" Anya remembered she still needed to put his plate away. And clean the puddles. And someone had tracked mud in earlier...

"Echoes of his Skill." Múdra raised a finger to her ear. "The Taliyaven blood in my veins is faint, but I can still hear echoes of their songs, especially when left by people I know. He was trying to eat unnoticed, wasn't he?"

"I...suppose so." Anya wasn't sure what Múdra was hinting at. She hadn't heard Dmitriy sing or say anything while he was eating.

"He does that when he's trying to hide. He'll call the shadows around him and almost fade from sight. You'd never see him if you didn't already know he was there."

Now Anya knew what Múdra was talking about, though she didn't quite understand. How many times had Dmitriy simply appeared somewhere, like a ghost? Anya assumed she hadn't been paying attention. But was there more to it? Some sort of magic?

"You know about the Talinae, don't you?"

"Of course. They appeared out of legends to help the High Houses win the war against Roche with their magic."

"Dmitriy has some of that magic. We're still trying to find out if he has Talinae blood, or if the Rochen people have their own type of Skill."

"The Talinae blood. Is that where his accent comes from?"

Múdra laughed. "*Nie!* The Talinae people sound almost like you and I. Their accent is not so noticeable. Dmitriy learned the common tongue from a man named Duren, and that's how Duren talks."

"So he just...picked up the accent?"

"Something like that. I'm not fully convinced it's not intentional on his part." Múdra gave Anya a sly grin. "Of course, Duren talks in that accent purely by choice."

"But it's not a Talinae accent? They usually sound like us?"

"*Áno.* We all speak different languages, but I've found they are very similar. I have friends who are trying to discover what happened between Roche and the Talinae, long before the High Houses came to Arromëre. We believe there is some connection between the Talinae, the Rochen, and the magic inside the land they have lived on for hundreds and hundreds of years."

Anya knew the tales of the people that once lived in Arromëre. They were full of fire and magic and song–things that only had a place in stories. The priests said the Rochen gods drove them out long ago, and it was only by sacrifices and bloodshed that the land would heal from their curses.

Once, Anya would have laughed at stories of song magic. But now that she had seen Arribor, she could understand. Arribor was full of magic. The green grass sparkled in the sunlight, and the ground practically *sang* with an eagerness to bring forth plenty. Anya could easily imagine magic residing here.

If there were ever a people or place incapable of magic, it was Roche. Nothing about the dark earth, the smoke-filled air, or the twisted faces of the priests spoke of a blessed land. If anything, the dead earth only proved Roche was cursed.

"Dmitriy is the only Rochen we know of with a Skill," Múdra continued. "He may have Talinae blood. Perhaps one ended up in Roche as a slave, and their child was sent to the Games. Or he may be Rochen through and through. Either way, he learned to use his Skill to protect himself, taking shadows to survive."

Anya imagined a young boy with Dmitriy's eyes, standing in the middle of a silencer arena and surrounded by men with swords. She thought of the missing finger on Dmitriy's hand, of the tattoos on his face, and of his limp. How many times had he faced death and survived?

How had someone raised in the silencer arenas become the quiet, gentle man she knew today? Who had taught him how to be kind?

"Are there Talinae here in Ozveny?"

"A few. Most are in their own land, rebuilding after the war. But there are a few in Arribor, using their Skills as best they can." Múdra tugged on a strand of her thick black hair. "You'll know them when you see them. They'll have hair unlike anything we have, and voices that sound like magic."

Anya couldn't imagine what that would sound like. The priests were angry that their *kráľ* had sided with the Talinae and won his throne through their help. The Talinae, they claimed, were everything the Rochen gods hated.

If the Rochen gods hated the Talinae so much, perhaps there was something good and wonderful about these mysterious people with singing magic.

"Knowing Dmitriy has a Skill gives me hope." Múdra pointed at Anya. "If Roche was once a beautiful place, it can be made such again. The Talinae can bring back the grass and flowers and beauty with their Skill. Wouldn't you like to see that?"

Could the barren plains of Roche, long bereft of trees and grass, fill with green again? Could the sinking pits of boiling water fade away and become firm ground? Could the tremors in the mountains, the ones the priests said came from the anger of the gods, fade into a memory of the past?

"I would love to see that," Anya agreed. "I can't imagine it. But I would love to see it."

"Then we pray to that end." Múdra pulled her cloak over her head, sending muddy drops onto her nose and the floor. "It's been a pleasure speaking with you, Miss Anya. We'll meet again someday, whether in this life or the next. Please think about becoming the *hrad's* Master of Music. I think you'd be a good one."

And with that, the Captain of the West Band was gone.

Anya rose to clean the floor before the next customer arrived. She needed to keep her hands busy while she pondered the day's conversations.

CHAPTER 14

ANYA SOLOVYOVA

OZVENY, THE ROYAL CITY OF ARRIBOR, SECOND AGE, 1998.

Ruženа had guests over for supper that night and insisted that Anya and her father join them. Anya felt they would be intruding, until she learned the guests were some of the very smugglers that would be taking them back to Roche.

Father quickly jumped into conversation, eager at the opportunity to speak Rochen again. The leader of the group, a man named Šimon Pevtsov, spoke with excitement about the journey, and it wasn't long before they had gone over every detail.

Their talk over the journey's dangers made Anya's head spin. Attacks from the giant eagles. Traveling through the Pathless Forest to save time. Guards at night to keep the jackals away. Detouring around Rochen towns to avoid being searched and the *Biblias* confiscated.

"It's risk all that, or else wait until summer. The Stryhaen Strait is too dangerous to travel through right now." Šimon shook his head. "There's still no word about our ship that went missing."

"It's my father's ship. If anyone can survive such weather, he can," Ruženа declared. "Don't call him dead yet. He's as stubborn as Ján when it comes to things like this. He'll make it back to land."

"And we believe in a God who protects," Šimon added. "But we can't sit and wait for news. I have a coterie willing to see us through the Pathless Forest and over the mountains. Unless you have news of the *Dawnwind*, we'll leave tomorrow as planned."

Their flight from Roche hadn't been smooth sailing. Even then, before the spring rain, the seas were rough with memories of winter. Would traveling through the mountains be much safer?

"Most of the snow should have melted by now," Šimon continued. "The mountain jackals will be hungry, but this coterie is recommended by Pavel Vetrov himself, so I trust they will be able to keep us safe."

Šimon clearly had no idea how much fear his words shot into Anya's heart. Hungry jackals? *Most* of the snow?

Anya looked at Father and found he was smiling, not at all concerned at the thought of hungry animals and treacherous mountain paths. Anya understood his longing to return to Roche, but she also wanted to arrive safely. They would be no help to Mother if they died in the mountains.

But how to tell Father? He wouldn't want to wait. The smugglers had their own reasons for traveling. She couldn't ask them to put their journey off for another week or two because she was afraid.

"I suppose Pavel isn't traveling with you, if he's sending a different coterie?" Kazimír had spoken little during the conversation, though Anya noticed he'd paid close attention.

Šimon shook his head. "*Nie.* He said he has to stay in Ozveny until the Nobility Council makes their decision about the Crown Warrior."

Ružena met her husband's eyes. "Any word on Dmitriy?"

"Officially, the Captain-General of the North Band has taken Dmitriy Vetrov into custody. He will not be released until the Eagle Council has made their verdict." Kazimír twirled his fork in his fingers. "*Unofficially,* he's probably with everyone at the West Band barracks tonight, listening to Ján's awful singing."

Anya had completely forgotten about the music at the West Band. Múdra's conversation about the Master of Music position and Talinae magic had chased everything else from Anya's head. If she'd remembered, it would have been nice to attend. It would be a shame to leave Arribor behind and never hear the music of her people.

"I imagine the attendance might be slim." Kazimír laughed. "Everyone is trying to become Ozveny's first Master of Music. I managed to catch one performance today, while bringing a message to Masha. The harpist made me want to cry, and not because they sounded good."

"Tomorrow is the last day." Ružena looked at Anya and smiled. "I forgot you play a few instruments. You should have tried. There's still time."

Anya shook her head. "I'm leaving tomorrow."

"But you don't want to go, do you?"

Anya met Father's glance. "I...I would like to go back and find Mother. We've already decided. I don't want to stay here alone or live off charity. I'll be fine going back."

"But if you are given the position, you'll make good income. You could easily rent your own place until you receive word from your family." Ružena rested her chin on her hands and leaned forward. "Would that be enough, Artyom Solovyov? Would you feel comfortable leaving your daughter behind in Ozveny in such a position?"

"I would." Father nodded. "What do you think, Anya?"

It was a good idea, but they had run out of time. The smugglers were leaving in the morning, and Anya wasn't guaranteed the position. If she failed, she would be left in Ozveny without her father, without a place to stay, and with only the kindness of others to survive.

"I would like that, but I don't have an instrument and I haven't practiced anything." Anya shrugged. "Perhaps if we'd thought about it sooner, it might have worked out."

"If you hadn't returned Dmitriy's *gusli*, you would have—" Ružena's eyes lit up. "*Nie, nie.* We can go back to get the *gusli* tonight! He won't mind. And I know who volunteered to judge the contestants. If they're willing to hear you play now, maybe we can get an answer in the morning before you leave!"

Even with a *gusli,* Anya still didn't have a song to play. She hadn't practiced anything with seriousness and had only revisited old favorites and tried to learn new ones from the music books Dmitriy had found.

Trying would be a waste of time. Going to the West Band would be a better use of her last evening in Arribor. She could enjoy the music, maybe say a final farewell and thank you to Dmitriy, then leave Arribor with happy memories. It might even give her some courage to take along on her dangerous journey.

Ružena leaned forward to stare Anya down. "Do you want to stay in Ozveny?"

Anya didn't know. She wanted to stay, but she wanted to see her mother again. She wanted to witness an Arriborn summer and see its beauty, but she also wanted to go home.

"I will try. If God wants me here in Ozveny, then so be it." Anya stood. "I'll leave it in His hands."

"Perfect!" Ružena jumped to her feet. "Kazimír, check the West Band barracks. I'll visit the nobles. I think most will be dining in the *hrad* anyway. Anya, get Dmitriy's *gusli* and meet me at the *hrad* gates."

"I'll clean up supper." Anya's father put an arm around her shoulders. "I will be praying for you. Do your best."

A few minutes later, Anya found herself trudging through dark streets in a warm mist. The thought of her unfinished supper made her stomach growl, but she hadn't dared eat the last of her food. She was rarely nervous when playing in front of people, but she'd never had such an important result hanging on her music.

If the judges didn't like her playing tonight, she would have to travel to Roche tomorrow.

If they approved, she would stay in Arribor and watch her Father leave.

If she messed up, she would travel to Roche.

If she played well, she might never see either of her parents again.

None of those outcomes pleased her, if she were honest. Being in charge of musical entertainment wasn't a bad occupation. But she was Rochen, not Arriborn. Why would they want someone from Roche overseeing their music?

She didn't want to cross the mountains, but she *did* want to see her mother again. And she didn't want to lose her father.

Anya stepped into a puddle hidden by the night shadows. Her right sock dampened. She considered turning around. It wasn't a good idea to take the *gusli* out in this sort of weather anyway.

Then again, she didn't want to be out in this weather either. Especially on the side of a mountain, hiding from giant eagles.

Anya continued on.

Dmitriy's house was dark and unlocked. The ashes in the kitchen were cold. Anya felt her way into the sitting room and knelt in front of the couch. Instead of wood and strings, her hand found only air underneath. She lay on the ground and peered into the dark but saw nothing.

She needed light. Thankfully, she knew where the tinder was kept and didn't need to explain her situation to the neighbors for fire.

Good evening. I'm Anya Solovyova, and I'm supposed to leave for Roche in the morning, but I don't want to go. So I'm going to try and become your Master of Music. I don't have an instrument, but your neighbor has a gusli *somewhere in his house. I'm going to borrow it while he's gone and under arrest because the Council wants to remove him from his position as Crown Warrior. Can I take a bit of fire from you? Oh, and do you maybe have an instrument I can borrow?*

As soon as she had a flame ready, Anya lit a candle and resumed her search. The small amount of light only confirmed her fear—the *gusli* was gone. She searched the room and found nothing. She searched the kitchen and found nothing. Not even a broken string.

She risked Dmitriy's study but saw only the desk and dust in an otherwise empty room. Even the crates were gone. The *Biblia* smugglers had probably already loaded them up in preparation to leave in the morning. Maybe one of the smugglers had wandered through the house, discovered the abandoned instrument, and decided to keep it?

Or maybe one of those nobles who wanted Dmitriy to lose his position had taken this opportunity to search and plunder the house? Anya squelched back into the kitchen and wondered if this was God's way of saying she was meant to return to Roche.

But that didn't feel right, even as she thought it. God had brought her here. He had brought her to Dmitriy's house. He'd brought Múdra to the bakery to tell her about the new position. He'd brought Ružena into her life to become her friend and to offer to gather the judges together so Anya could play for them.

Anya would find *something*. She liked the *gusli* best, but she could play other instruments. The previous owners of this house had owned a *gusli*, and musicians rarely owned only one instrument. Perhaps she could find another in this house.

But she needed to hurry.

Anya ran up the stairs, taking two at a time. There were still three chests that she hadn't had time to go through. Perhaps there was a *píšťalka* or a harp or something. Even a harp with missing strings would do. She could pick a song that didn't require those strings.

She could stand up in front of those judges and do nothing but *sing*, if she had to. Maybe she was worrying too much. All she had to do was show she had an ear for music.

The first chest held nothing but filthy, mouse-eaten cloaks. Had she still been employed by Dmitriy, Anya wouldn't have even bothered showing them to him. The second chest contained dusty books. A few might have been music books, but Anya wasn't interested.

"Oh God, please, let this one have something," Anya whispered, throwing open the last chest. She sneezed as a cloud of dust rose in the air, then raised the candle to peer inside.

Dresses and boots. Anya grabbed handfuls of fabric and embroidery, throwing them onto the floor beside her. Only when there was a solitary boot left on the floor of the chest did she accept it didn't contain an instrument.

Not even a little *píšťalka.* Anya rose to her feet. She didn't like wind instruments much, but she could play one—as long as there actually was one to play.

The desire to kick at the pile of musty dresses and declare the entire night a failure was strong. Anya stared at the mess she had made, then remembered she had tracked wet footprints all over the house.

She should probably give up and focus on cleaning the house. It wouldn't be polite to leave Dmitriy with a messy floor to come home to. Unless losing his position also made him lose his house? Or perhaps the Nobility Council would try to have him arrested and imprisoned while they were at it?

Anya rose and stood in the hallway for a moment. If Dmitriy was going to lose the house, she would leave the mess for whoever received it next—a tiny act of revenge against the Nobility Council.

You think you can get rid of Dmitriy? Well, have fun cleaning his house. I made quite a mess for you. Hopefully you like mouse-eaten dresses and dusty books.

Not a bad farewell. Anya went to her old bedroom and opened the door. The bed was still there, missing the blankets that Dmitriy had brought to Ružena's. He'd even brought their clothes over. How many trips had he had to make? Or had he somehow bundled everything together and managed it all in one go?

Anya would have liked to see that. She would pray he kept his position. Maybe she could write to Ružena once she reached Roche and ask how things had gone.

She continued down the hall until she stood in front of Dmitriy's room. It had an ordinary door like the others. If Anya had to guess, the bedroom was as barren and sad as the rest of the house. A bed, for certain. Blankets, hopefully. Dmitriy probably kept his clothes in something, because they never looked horribly wrinkled. Sometimes he would leave cloaks and shirts on the kitchen table, and Anya would wash them and hang them up. Eventually, they would disappear.

Anya placed her hand on the door. "Goodbye, Dmitriy. Thanks for your kindness. I hope God blesses you in return."

The door rocked open an inch, and Anya pulled her hand away. Dmitriy must not have closed the door all the way. She should shut it and leave. The rain was growing heavier, and she still had to find her way to the *hrad* gates and tell Ružena she had nothing to play.

Anya opened the door and walked inside the bedroom. Her boots landed on something soft, and she looked down to see blankets spread out across the floor like a garden of colors. A bed in one corner overflowed with blankets and pillows that spilled onto the floor. Cloaks of all kinds were nailed along the walls, and clothes were stacked and draped across the back of a line of chairs. A desk held towers of books and piles of papers. One corner held cleaning supplies and a rusty sword. A lute leaned in another corner, and Anya's *gusli* lay below it, still wrapped in the blanket she'd put it in.

She hadn't expected so much *stuff.* At first glance, the room was chaos, and Anya's fingers itched to fold the blankets and hang the clothes. But as she tiptoed her way across the floor to the *gusli*, she changed her mind.

Dmitriy had been born as a slave in Roche. He had been trained to fight from a young age and win money for his masters. The tattoos on his face meant he had accomplished numerous feats worthy of remembrance.

If Anya had to guess, he hadn't come to Arribor as a child. He would have spent much of his life living in the cells and stench of silencer arenas. As a slave, he would have owned nothing. Now Dmitriy had a place of his own, with things of his own to keep inside. It was a safe place. A comfortable place. He'd even asked that no one else go inside, and Anya had violated that wish.

She looked over her shoulder, but Dmitriy was not there. The candlelight shadows were empty. She was the only one in the room. An intruder.

Anya picked up the *gusli* and made sure it hadn't been damaged. All the strings were still in place. No dents or scrapes. She would need to tune it, but that wasn't a surprise.

"I'm going to return everything," Anya whispered, grabbing a cloak from a nearby chair. "I promise." She wrapped the *gusli* back in the blanket, then wrapped the bundle in the cloak for extra protection.

Maybe she should leave a note, just in case? Anya decided it couldn't hurt. She poked through the piles of papers on the desk but couldn't find a pen. By her reasoning, there *should* be something to write with, since an inkwell sat on top of the desk beside a cup full of dead roses.

Anya knew that brown cup. She'd put those flowers in it. Her thank-you note was still resting beside them. Dmitriy had kept her note. And the roses. The water inside the cup was fairly fresh, which meant he'd been pouring more water in. They'd still died, but that was normal.

But he'd tried to make them last as long as he could. That was kind of him.

Anya placed the dead bouquet in the middle of the desk and set her old note in front of them. If Dmitriy made it back before she could return everything, he would notice the missing *gusli,* see this, and hopefully understand what had happened.

She grabbed her instrument bundle and fled the room.

Chapter 15

Anya Solovyova

Ozveny, the Royal City of Arribor, Second Age, 1998.

Anya didn't believe in ghosts. She liked to think she wasn't normally afraid of things. (Silencers appearing out of the shadows would surely make *anyone* panic and did not count as things that made her fearful.)

But the Ozveny *hrad* was absolutely terrifying at night. Wind pulled at the strands of ivy, and the leaves pattered across the stone walls. Golden light flickered behind some of the windows, while others remained dark. Anya could only hear the patter of rain on stone. If someone was behind her, she would never know.

Ružena led the way from the gates to a side door with the confidence of someone who was right where they meant to be. Anya could only follow and avoid stepping in puddles, her precious bundle wrapped in her arms.

Inside the *hrad,* the darkness continued but the sound of rain faded. A guard stood right inside the door, a dying torch fixed into the wall by his shoulder. He took their names and their cloaks and bowed politely to Ružena as she passed. Anya wondered if he would have killed them if Ružena weren't someone important enough to enter the *hrad* at night.

"It's not far," Ružena said, her voice echoing strangely against the stone walls. "Do you know what you're going to play?"

Anya hadn't thought that far ahead. Her toes were completely soaked. The *gusli* still needed to be tuned. There was still mud on the floor in Dmitriy's house that she should clean up.

Ružena led her into a large room lit with a roaring fire. A long, empty table filled the center of the room, indicating the place was chiefly used for dining. Six people sat on chairs near the fireplace, talking softly. A seventh figure stood by the fire, adding another log to the flames.

The talking stopped when Ružena closed the door. "I brought her," she said.

"I hope she's as good as you say she is," a woman's voice snapped from across the empty table. "You've dragged me away from my party, so this better be worth it."

"I think you'll be satisfied, Lady Kos." Ružena led Anya closer to the semicircle of strangers. "May I present my friend, Anya Solovyova."

"That's not an Arriborn name," someone said.

"It sounds Rochen," a man with a thin golden crown said. "Not that I'm very familiar with Rochen names. If I ever get to travel there someday, perhaps I might learn more about its people. But *nie*. It's too dangerous for the *kráľ* to travel. I might—"

"She is from Roche," Ružena interrupted. "Anya arrived with the *Biblia* smugglers."

Anya froze. No one laughed. No one called for guards to throw her into prison. No one demanded she prove her loyalty to the Rochen gods. The *kráľ* of Arribor merely looked her in the eyes and grinned, rather impishly.

Could someone truly mention the *Biblia* in the presence of royalty and not lose their lives? What a place Arribor was!

"I look forward to hearing what she plays." The young *kráľ* settled back into his chair. The person by the fire stepped a little closer, and Anya saw it was a woman with hair red as the flames themselves. A sword rested on each hip, much like the two swords Dmitriy carried. "Do we still have our bet, Masha?" the *kráľ* asked her.

"I made no such promise," Masha said. She stood behind the *kráľ* like a protective blaze, tall and powerful. Her voice was full of strength and laughter and a hint of something more. Was this the Skill that Múdra had mentioned? Did this woman have Talinae blood?

Ružena brought Anya a chair from the table, and Anya sat and unwrapped the *gusli*. Leaving the cloak and the blanket in a pile at her feet, she began to tune the instrument.

But what to play?

Something to bring the sharp woman to tears?

Something to make the *kráľ* laugh?

Something to chisel softness into the red-haired woman's posture?

Anya set her fingers on the strings. "Thank you for coming to listen to me tonight," she said, her eyes on the instrument. "I know you didn't have to. I hope I can make your sacrifice worth the while."

God, bless my music.

She plucked the first string. This song was her mother's favorite—a tune that accompanied many of the *Žalms* they sang. Anya only played it when the inn was empty and the risk of being recognized as a Christian was all but gone. Tonight, she could play it without fear.

And her favorite part? She could easily weave this song right into the next. If she played Mother's favorite, it was only fair she play one Father loved as well.

Artyom Solovyov loved songs that told stories, and this one he sang often. Anya had heard it many times these past few weeks as he'd planted and weeded in Dmitriy's garden.

Though it was in Rochen, Anya didn't dare try to translate words in the middle of a song. She merely sang in her own language and hoped the Arriborn people would appreciate the music even when the lyrics couldn't be understood.

As she neared the end of the second song, a passage of notes reminded her of one of the Arriborn songs she had practiced from

Dmitriy's music books. It spoke of the beauty of Arribor, of places Anya wished she had time to find and visit. She changed the tune, blending them, then began a third song, praying her memory had collected all the words correctly.

"The birds call out the coming dawn,

soft mist is in the air,

And whispering trees move in the breeze

as I offer up this prayer.

Open doors show morning lights.

The fire still lies cold.

And the night owl calls one last farewell

into the sunrise gold."

Anya didn't dare look up. Back home, she would sit back and smile at customers and watch them eat and dance and enjoy her music. But they were people just like her. They only wanted a good song.

If she looked up, if she lost her nerve or lost the song, tomorrow would see her climbing into a wagon to travel back to Roche. She would leave behind the gardens and fields and flowers of Arribor. She would leave this land that had already claimed her heart.

"Stormy winds wail up the way
and springtime showers fall.
And the mountain pines reach to the skies
since mossy stones recall.

Had a gusli *made of gold.*
Every string did shine,
Like summer sun on water runs
and catches in your eye.

Sit on a stone on a winter's day
and listen to the snow.
Wishes, songs, they dance along,
from words lost long ago.

This quiet home's a calling me.
It's here I'll live my life.
Until I breathe my last full breath
and never know more strife."

She finished with her favorite ending, one she often used for slower, more thoughtful songs. It begged listeners to contemplate the words as she dragged the notes out, letting the last string ring deep.

Only when the music faded did she risk looking up. Ružena stood beside the *kráľ*, and their smiles were nearly identical. The red-haired woman behind them stood still like a statue. Anya didn't dare look at the others.

No one spoke.

Then the woman with the swords, Masha, moved to the shadows by the side of the fireplace and picked up a small harp. She carried it to Anya and held it out. "Can you play the harp?" Her voice was gentle, and Anya felt the question was not a challenge but mere curiosity.

The harp was worn from years of use, and the strings were already tuned. Anya knew exactly what she would play and began a well-loved Rochen dance tune. Her fingers darted over the strings, and she could almost imagine she was back at the *Quiet Waters*. Once she finished, Vera would stomp in from the kitchen and beg for another.

"Beautiful," Masha said when Anya stopped playing. "You have a gift. Skill worthy of a Talinae master of old." She took the harp and faced the others. "You know where my vote lies. That is all I will say."

"I think I agree with Masha. My vote is for the Rochen woman with the *gusli*." The *kráľ* spun his crown around a finger. "I don't even need to hear the others tomorrow. I doubt my mind could be changed, unless someone is able to play the fiddle with their feet."

Ružena laughed. No one else did.

"And my vote counts twice, since I'm the *kráľ*."

"That will be taken into account." A woman wiped her eyes. "We can conduct the other auditions without you."

Anya couldn't wait for them to continue through tomorrow. She needed her answer *now.* If they weren't going to make their decision until everyone had performed, Anya's attempt had been a waste of time.

She'd invaded Dmitriy's house a second time, trespassed into his bedroom, run through the *hrad* in the rain, and risked playing before the *kráľ*, all for nothing.

"She has my vote," said another voice. A man leaned back in his chair, hands resting on his ample stomach. "I won't be here tomorrow, either."

"You only want an excuse to spend tomorrow at Eliška's party!" The *kráľ* laughed.

"I'm finished listening to music for hours on end. The Nobility Council is tired of taking the blame for disgruntled dancers. Just give her the position now and save us all."

Anya sat in her chair, *gusli* in her lap, and wondered if she would ever feel worthy of a position given to her because people wanted to go to a party instead of faithfully listen to everyone interested in the role.

"If she does a poor job, people will continue to complain. Then we'll have to do this again in a month or two." One of the women blew out a sigh. "But...we'll receive complaints no matter what. I'll give her my vote, then. And I won't be here tomorrow, either. I've got better things to do."

The woman stood, wrapped a cloak around her shoulders, and left without another word.

"Is anyone opposed to offering Miss Solovyova the position right now?" the *kráľ* asked.

No one spoke.

"I suppose we'll need to have the official paperwork drawn up tomorrow. But Miss Vávrová, you'll gather all the information you need, correct?"

A young woman nodded. "*Áno.* I'll get it ready to submit to the Council in the morning. I'll need her name, her place of residence, and the gift she would like to request. Once the Council has approved, I can submit a payment contract for her weekly allowance."

"You did it!" Ružena threw her arms around Anya, nearly knocking the *gusli* to the ground. "I knew you would impress them. Your playing is even better than I expected. You really do have a gift!"

Anya swallowed down a defense, a denial, and a declaration of her unworthiness. It was over. She had a position in the *hrad.* She could stay in Arribor. She would be working, supporting herself. And she had a place to stay.

Well, almost. She still needed to arrange for housing. She could probably stay with Ružena a little longer, until she saved a bit of money. Surely someone would willingly rent a room or two to the official Master of Music.

"What of your gift?" The *kráľ* rose and approached Anya. His smile was infectious, and Anya wondered how he and the quieter Dmitriy had met and become friends. "The Nobility Council promised to grant one request. I think they were doubtful people would apply unless they got something special out of it. But I disagree. A musician plays because they love music. And a Master of Music must treat their position seriously. I'm certain you will be worthy of the title."

But what gift should she ask for? Asking for a place to stay would sound too vague. Should she ask for a room in the *hrad*? Some additional money so she could find a place of her own right away? How much would a house cost? She didn't need something big, like the grand homes Ružena and Dmitriy lived in. Just a little place.

Then again, Dmitriy had been gifted the large house. Maybe she could find another one in the city that needed someone to clean it up and make it a home.

"The Nobility Council made it clear they could not bestow the throne, if you were thinking of asking for my crown." The *kráľ* touched the circlet on his head. "I made sure they clarified that before we made the announcement. Just in case they were thinking of trying to remove me. Again."

Anya already disliked the Nobility Council. If the *kráľ* spoke ill of them, perhaps it wasn't only her one-sided opinion based on their treatment of Dmitriy.

"They said they would grant a request," Anya repeated. "But they can't give anyone the throne. What are the other conditions?"

She had an idea. It was probably an awful, stupid idea. But the more she learned about the Nobility Council, the more annoyed she became. The thought of annoying them in return grew stronger by the minute.

It might cost her a nice place to stay. It might cost her request being fulfilled at all. But it would be nice to pay Dmitriy back for his kindness, and the thought of bothering the Nobility Council made it even more enticing.

"*Welllllll...*" The *kráľ* tilted his head back. "Múdra made sure the chosen Master must be able to play at least one instrument. Someone said they also needed to be able to sing, but I can't remember if that was agreed upon or not. You sing well, so I don't think it matters if that part is on the contract or not."

"*Nie.* What else can't the Council offer as a gift? Did they provide a list?"

"I don't think so." The *kráľ* looked at Ružena. "What else did they say?"

"Nothing that excludes a Rochen from taking the position." Ružena smiled. "I wouldn't have suggested it to you otherwise."

"But what can I ask for? Or what *can't* I ask for?"

"They said you can't have Ján's throne, so that's out. They put a limit on money, though the amount was not revealed on the announcement."

Ján made a strange face, clearly directed at Anya. "Please don't tell me you want to ask for money?"

Anya shook her head.

"Good! I was afraid you were going to be terribly boring. You should ask for my firstborn child. That should give the Nobility Council a surprise."

"I have an even better idea." Anya grinned back at the *kráľ*. "I want to request the Nobility Council to leave Dmitriy Vetrov alone and let him remain by your side in peace."

Chapter 16

Anya Solovyova

Ozveny, the Royal City of Arribor, Second Age, 1998.

Anya watched Father leave on a morning heavy with the promise of rain. She stood on Ružena's front porch and let her tears fall as he climbed into one of the laden wagons and rattled off into the mist. She waited, long after the sound of hooves on stone was gone, until the rain began to fall and Ružena dragged her back into the house.

"Did I do the right thing?" she asked as Ružena wiped rain off her face with her apron.

"Did you do the right thing?" Ružena repeated. "How should I know?"

"Should I have gone with my father?"

Ružena shrugged. "You didn't want to cross the mountains. God provided a way for you to stay. If you're meant to return to

Roche, then it'll happen someday. In the meantime, you're in charge of music at the *hrad.* If you put the same dedication into that as you've done with everything else here in Ozveny, you'll be fine."

The thought of returning to the *hrad* was rather terrifying. Anya still didn't know if the Nobility Council would accept her request. What if it angered them and they refused to give her the position? She would be jobless, homeless, and far away from her family—exactly what she had hoped to avoid.

All for a silencer.

She should have asked for a place to stay. Money for a house. Something that would ensure her future would be more secure. Dmitriy had powerful friends. He didn't need some random woman putting her lot in with him.

"You did a good thing," Ružena finally said. "Now we just need to see it through to the end. Let's clean up breakfast and head up to the *hrad.* You need to be ready in case the Nobility Council calls for you."

Anya didn't want to stand before the Nobility Council. She wanted some important-looking person to hand her a slip of paper that said Dmitriy would be left alone and as the new Master of Music, she could have her pick of any empty bedroom in the *hrad.*

But things rarely turned out so easy. No doubt the Council would argue and debate. They would call Anya in only to insult her to her face. They might even accuse her of being a Rochen spy. She would be thrown into prison.

Ružena did not seem to have that same concern. She chatted as they cleaned the kitchen after breakfast, then offered to braid

Anya's hair before they left for the *hrad.* Anya was too nervous to refuse.

When they finally left the house to begin the trek to the *hrad,* the rain had slowed to a heavy mist. Bright beams of light occasionally cracked through as if the sun was trying to win a losing battle.

At least the *hrad* was a livelier place in the daytime. People filled the courtyard, dodging puddles and hurrying through their errands. Even the hallways were alight with blazing torches, open doors and windows, and cheerful smiles. Perhaps Anya would become yet another face in the constant stream of people rushing back and forth with important jobs to do.

She would enjoy that.

Ružena turned and entered a long hallway lined with thick rugs and large windows. Signs of wear showed in the middle of the rugs, marking where people usually walked.

"This is the hallway that leads to the Room of the Eagles," Ružena explained. "All the various Arriborn councils meet here. It's also where Dmitriy fought his way through half of the North Band warriors to rescue the *kráľovná.*"

No wonder the Nobility Council feared Dmitriy. They were reminded of what he could do every time they held a meeting. And now Anya found herself wondering if the rugs had been stained with blood. Who had been the one tasked with cleaning the hallway after the fight?

Two guards stood before a pair of double doors, and they bowed when Ružena approached. "Lady Rehák."

"Has the Council asked for Anya Solovyova?"

"*Nie.*"

Ružena gestured to a small bench. "Take a seat and don't go anywhere. If the Council wants to talk to you, they'll send someone."

"What about you?"

Ružena turned to the door. "I'm part of the Nobility Council, and I'm afraid I'm running late."

When the guards opened one of the doors, Anya caught a glimpse of a long table surrounded by great eagle statues. The door closed, swallowing Ružena and leaving Anya alone with two guards.

She took a seat and waited. Every so often, she heard raised voices, but mostly, she heard nothing but her own heartbeat. The guards did not speak, and she did not try to talk to them.

Maybe facing the giant eagles of the Narravian Mountains would have been easier. She should have taken her chances with the jackals.

God, give me peace. I can't stand this waiting.

Anya rose and walked down the hall, turning back before the hallway curved and concealed her from sight of the doors. She wasn't leaving, only stretching her legs. If she didn't move, her fears and concerns would build.

She stopped in front of one of the windows and peered out, examining the mist-covered garden below. Father would have loved exploring the *hrad* gardens. If he had stayed, perhaps she could have used her position to allow him entrance. Even if he wasn't the one responsible for the care, he would still enjoy walking the paths and looking at the flowers.

Anya made a few passes along the hallway, sometimes walking the worn path, sometimes traversing the edges of the rugs. She stopped at a spot where something dark poked out from under the fabric and pulled up the corner of the rug. An old stain discolored the stone.

Blood.

Had no one bothered to clean the hallway after the fight? Or was this the best they'd been able to manage? Anya pulled the rug up further to reveal more stains—some darker, some lighter.

This was the royal *hrad.* This was the hallway to the great Room of the Eagles. And *this* was the best cleaning job they could get?

Anya *tsked.* This was a disaster.

"Miss Solovyova?"

Anya turned to see the sharp-toned woman from last night—one of the judges for the Master of Music position. And apparently one of the Nobility Council members.

So this was the moment. Anya dropped the rug and kicked it back into place. "*Áno?*"

"The Nobility Council has written up your contract, if you would sign it in my presence for me to return to them."

Anya accepted the paper, smudging one of the lines. She smiled apologetically and began reading.

In the year 1998 of the second age, in the seventh year of the reign of Kráľ Ján Drobný, has Anya Solovyova been commissioned as the Master of Music in the hrad. *She will be required to fulfill the tasks as listed below, and payment for her services will be issued regularly upon the last day of each week.*

Anya scanned the list of duties, noting the pay seemed fair. She had no problem performing before crowds, and hiring minstrels and groups to play for parties and festivals was something she would enjoy. The position was a decent fit with her own skills.

But what about the request?

In opening this position, the Nobility Council has promised to fulfill one request of the chosen applicant. The given request, asking for leniency on the actions of Dmitriy Vetrov, has been received and accepted. So long as Anya Solovyova resides in the position of Master of Music, the Nobility Council will cease from making accusations against Dmitriy Vetrov.

Below the final paragraph were scrawled a number of signatures. Anya didn't even try to make out any of the names. But the message was clear: Dmitriy would be safe for now. If Anya lost or left her position, the Council might bring up his past again. She didn't dare complain.

She took the offered pen and wrote her name. It was in Rochen, but hopefully no one would contest that. "Do you need anything else?"

"*Nie.* We'll send a copy to your current place of residence. Your duties will begin at the start of the week. You will report to the *hrad* mistress, Lady Poduska."

The councilwoman took the paper and left, marching down the middle of the rug to the guarded doors. Anya waited until she was back in the Room of the Eagles before continuing her investigation of the bloodstains.

It wasn't until the Council was released and a horde of nobles and warriors streamed through the hallway that Anya realized all her worrying had been for nothing. They had given her a slip of paper and moved on. No charges. No threat of prison. Not even a welcome.

As she stood to the side and watched the unfamiliar faces pass by, many didn't even bother to look at her. Well, that would quickly become a thing of the past. She was the Master of Music. Soon, everyone would know her name.

"Well, that went well!" Ružena slid up behind Anya and hooked an arm around her waist. "I think we should hold a celebration at my house, don't you? Look outside! The sun's finally coming out. Maybe we can have supper in the back garden tonight. I'll see if I can dig out some *slivovitz.*"

It was settled. Anya had a job as well as someone she could call a friend and who didn't see her as a burden. She had things to do and all the time in the world to do them.

"A party sounds lovely," Anya replied. "Can I provide the music?"

"I expect nothing but the best from our Master of Music. I will be the envy of all Ozveny, receiving your first public performance!"

Anya was already planning the coming weeks. She would create a list of minstrels who lived in Ozveny. There had to be some sort of music school that would be willing to play in the *hrad.* The West Band apparently had a lot of musicians who attended, and she might find some talent worthy to set before the *kráľ.*

She would need her own set of instruments, of course. And Dmitriy had mentioned a *hrad* library that contained music books. If she was going to play before a chiefly Arriborn audience, she would need to build up her repertoire of Arriborn songs.

"You're smiling," Ružena teased. "Do you really like parties that much?"

"Just thinking about what I'm going to play."

The sun was shining when they left the *hrad* behind and began the walk to Ružena's house. Puddles gleamed blue, casting memories of sunbeams into the air. Anya looked up at the brilliant sky and wondered how she could have ever agreed to leave Arribor.

If only her family was with her, she would be perfectly content.

When they reached the house, Ružena hurried to the kitchen to begin the preparations for a grand party. Anya went to the back garden and took a seat on one of the benches. She could see Father's handiwork all around her. The neat rows of carefully weeded flowers, the dead leaves and growth from winter all neatly burned, and the polished steps winding a merry path through the flower beds.

"Thank you, God," Anya said aloud. She could have shouted it if she wanted to. No one would arrest her for saying such things.

"Indeed. Thank ye, God."

The voice was Dmitriy's. Anya squeaked in surprise as the Crown Warrior stepped away from the gate and entered the garden.

"You need to stop doing that," Anya scolded. "It scares me every time!"

"Ah'm sorry." Dmitriy lowered his head. "Ah just got here."

"So you weren't using your magic to sneak up on me?"

"*Nie.*"

Anya gestured to the sword on his back. "Well, maybe rattle your swords a little or trip on something so I can hear you coming. Seeing you fall on your face would be better than watching you appear out of the shadows like a ghost."

Dmitriy smiled, and Anya realized his handkerchief was gone. She hadn't even noticed at first. His tattoos were visible now, but a bit of stubble was beginning to cover them. Faint scars on his cheeks marked where the handkerchief had once cut into his skin.

"I don't think I've ever seen you smile," Anya added. Her cheeks burned, but she managed to deliver the next line without a stutter. "It looks nice, when you do that."

"Ah came here tae thank ye fer standin' up fer me before the Nobility Council. Ján said they were goin' tae take mae cloak fer sure." Dmitriy sat beside her on the bench. "Ah'd probably get it back eventually, but not without a fight."

"Do they really hate you because you fought the North Band?"

Dmitriy shrugged. "Arriborn politics. The old Captain of the North Band was going tae kill the *kráľovná.* Many in Arribor supported it. Some are angry Ah stopped them. Others just don't like that Ah'm from Roche. Perhaps some simply fear a sword they can't control."

"You're more than a sword." Anya put a hand on his shoulder. Dmitriy didn't flinch, but he did watch her for a moment before turning to study the garden.

"Yer father does good work. Mae garden is a different place. And the house. Ah cannae thank ye enough fer cleanin' everything."

Anya remembered the floor and the chaos upstairs. "And I made a huge mess last night! I'm so sorry. I was looking for the *gusli.*"

"And ye found it?"

"...*Áno*..." Anya winced. "I'm sorry about that. I shouldn't have gone into your room." Should she say something else? Compliment his decorating? Try to apologize more? Promise she would never invade his house again? "I saw you kept the roses I gave you."

"Ah'm sorry Ah couldn't keep them alive. Ah donnae 'ave a skill for growin' things, not like yer father."

"They would die eventually, no matter what you did. The only way to keep them forever is to dry and press them. Mother did that whenever Father managed to grow something outside the inn." Anya swallowed at the memory. It seemed to stick in her throat, and tears sprung to her eyes. "She would hang them from the rafters in the kitchen. She said they brightened up the place."

"Sounds beautiful."

"I can show you how do that, if you'd like."

Dmitriy tilted his head back, and a small smile spread across his lips. "Ah think Ah'd like that."

Anya blushed.

"The West Band is going have a celebration tomorrow. Lots of music and *pivo* and *pirohy*. Ah'd like tae take ye, if ye'll come. Lots of people Ah want ye tae meet."

Over the years of working at *Quiet Waters*, Anya had received interest from all sorts of people. Some comments were casual jokes told over one-too-many drinks; others were serious offers, meant to take her away from a home and family she knew well. Anya had turned down all of them almost instantly.

But this one, if it was an offer, was worth considering.

Anya risked looking up. "Careful. It sounds like you want to court me."

Dmitriy held out a hand. "May Ah?"

Footsteps clattered on the front porch, and Ružena rushed out into the garden, her bare feet slapping on stone. "Anya! Anya! I have news!"

"News?"

"My father's ship! It arrived in Stormport a few days ago. Your mother is aboard!" Ružena grabbed Anya's hands and yanked her to her feet. "They're both alive and well!"

"She's alive? And in Arribor?"

"*Áno!* She's on her way to Ozveny now. My father sent a message ahead." Ružena prodded Dmitriy on the shin with a toe. "You might want to wait until Anya's parents are back before you try courting her."

Dmitriy didn't so much as blush. "Ah understand. Ah will wait."

"But what about Father? He's on his way to Roche! He doesn't know the ship survived." Anya nearly ran out the gate. "We have to let him know!"

"There's already a messenger riding out to catch the smugglers with the news. You should be united with your family in a day or two." Ružena held up a finger. "Until then, I will be your guardian. And I say no more unsupervised conduct. Come now, into the kitchen, both of you. I think half the West Band's planning to attend tonight and meet the new Master of Music, and I need your help cooking enough soup to feed everyone."

"Very well." Anya held out a hand to Dmitriy. "It looks like I'm meeting some of your friends sooner than expected."

"An' Ah'll meet yer mother." Dmitriy took Anya's hand, stood, then bowed. "Perhaps Ah'll get a proper introduction this time, instead o' findin' ye in mae garden or somewhere else ye're not supposed tae be."

"I'll do my best." Anya squeezed his hand. "But I seem to have made a habit of being found in places I shouldn't be. Quite like someone else I know. You better be careful, or I might hit you with an instrument someday."

Dmitriy threw his head back and laughed. His voice was soft and quiet, but something wild rang in every word he spoke. "Ah'm Dmitriy Vetrov, the Crown Warrior of Arribor. Ah sing tae the shadows an' fear nothing–except one high an' mighty Master of Music. She strikes fear in mae very heart!"

Anya leaned closer. "And if you're not careful, I'll be doing it for the rest of our lives."

Dokončené.

We hope you enjoyed *The Crown Warrior of Arribor* by Helena Š. George! If you did, please consider leaving a review on your favorite review sites. It is a great help to authors!

Glossary

Anna Múdra (an-NA MOO-dra): Arriborn. Captain of the West Band. Supports the *Bibla* smugglers and is an avid music lover.

Anya Solovyova (AHN-yah SOLL-ov-YOV-ah): Rochen. Persecuted Christian on the run. Talented musician (prefers the *gusli* most).

Artyom Solovyov (art-YOOM SOLL-ov-yov): Rochen. Owner of *Quiet Waters* inn. Persecuted Christian on the run. Married to Galina.

Dmitriy Vetrov (de-MEET-tree veh-TROV): Rochen. Crown Warrior to Ján Drobný. Previously a silencer slave before earning his freedom and becoming a Christian during the Red War.

Galina Solovyov (GAL-in-ah SOLL-ov-YOV-ah): Rochen. Cook at *Quiet Waters* inn. Persecuted Christian on the run.

Ján Drobný (YAWN DROB-knee): Arribor. Kráľ of Arriborn. Recently attained his throne during the Red War.

Kazimír Rehák (kah-ZUH-meer REE-hack): Arriborn. West Band warrior. Married to Ružena.

Lujza (LOO-ee-zah): Arriborn. Ex-thief. Now works in a bakery in Ozveny.

Masha Blackburn (MAH-sha BLACK-burn): Taliyaven. Crown Warrior to Ján Drobný. A Skilled singer and harpist.

Ružena Rehák (roo-SHEE-nah REE-hack): Arriborn. Noblewoman. Previous West Band warrior. Sister to Ján, married to Kazimir.

Sevastyan Usenko (see-VAST-yan you-SHEN-co): Rochen. The Rochen *kráľ*, newly crowned during the Red War. Trying to bring peace between Roche and her neighbors with the hope of restoring the land.

Šimon Pevtsov (SHI-mon PEHVT-sov): Taliyaven. Lives in Roche as a *Biblia* smuggler.

Vera Solovyova (VEE-rah SOLL-ov-YOV-ah): Rochen. A young Christian woman, she gave her life for her faith. Killed at the raid on *Quiet Waters.*

Yekaterina (YEE-kat-er-EE-nah): Rochen. Noblewoman. A persecuted Christian on the run, she lost her entire family during the raid on *Quiet Waters* inn.

Yuli (YOO-lee): Rochen. Slave to the high priest in the town of Sochi. He spies around to find Christians living in his city.

Dictionary

Áno - yes

Biblia - Bible

Hrad - castle

Kráľ - king

Kráľovná - queen

Nie - no

Pirohy - dumpling, commonly filled with potato

Píšťalka - a small flute or whistle

Pivo - beer

Slivovitz - strong plum brandy

Víno - wine

Žalm - psalm

Acknowledgements

This book was dedicated to my mom, and rightfully so. During the slogs and doldrums of writing a huge fantasy series, she was right there beside me—living out her own "daily grind" as she managed a family and a farm, all while taking care of herself and striving for her own goals of health and fitness. As I struggled with writing a few pages a night, she quietly persevered and read a few pages a night, even when she was tired and ready for bed. I cannot thank her enough for her love, her encouragement, and her example.

(Mom, here's one more book for you to read—but at least it's shorter and contains your favorite character. I love you!)

But thanks must also go to Sarah Rodecker, my dearest friend, my co-writer, my business partner, and general partner in crime. She kept me on track, helped me with brainstorming, shared my love for this story, and held no judgement when I (also known as Ms-I-Hate-Romantasy) announced that I had an idea for a romantasy novella.

I also need to thank Denica McCall for doing the edits on *Crown Warrior*. It was so nice doing the final proof read and finding almost nothing else that needed to change. This book is better because of your work!

Lastly, thanks to God for giving me this love and passion for stories, and putting these people and opportunities in my life. Solo Deo Gloria!

About the Author

HELENA Š. GEORGE is an author, musician, and horsewoman. She began her publishing journey in 2020, and co-founded The Order of the Pen Press. When she isn't working with books, she can be found camping in the mountains with her horses, playing the mandolin and dreaming up new adventures.

Enjoy this story? Check out the rest of our catalogue at orderofthepenpress.com/s/shop

The Pirate Hunter Chronicles

The Red War Annals

Mossyhollow Mysteries

Short Story Anthology

www.ingramcontent.com/pod-product-compliance
Lightning Source LLC
LaVergne TN
LVHW090525110826
845146LV00003B/982

* 9 7 9 8 9 9 5 1 2 1 6 0 2 *